Ezra
Exposed

Ezra Exposed

AMY E. FELDMAN

BLACK STONE PUBLISHING

Printed in the United States of America

First edition: 2022
ISBN 979-8-200-79748-6
Juvenile Fiction / Technology / General

Version 1

CIP data for this book is available
from the Library of Congress

Blackstone Publishing
31 Mistletoe Rd.
Ashland, OR 97520

www.BlackstonePublishing.com

To Paul Epstein, Ray Feldman,
and Len Feldman, three wonderful dads,
whose love means the world to their children,
and
to my wonderful children,
who are my world

Contents

Finally

"Tell me you didn't go to school like that."

It was the very first thing Dad said when Mom and me and Emmie scooched into the booth at Elly Fants, where he'd been waiting for us.

I made a face. "Yeah, Mom picked out this shirt. I told her it was too hot to wear. I was sweaty all day."

"Not the shirt. The 'stache, dude."

Oh. Right. I had gotten up that morning before everyone else and found the Sharpie Mom used to label our clothes. So what could I do?

I mean, it's not like I could grow an actual mustache yet. But that didn't mean I couldn't try it on to see how it would look. It would look great, in case you were wondering, although I knew it would take three days for the Sharpie to wear off. "Yeah. Ms. Robinson loved it."

"Really?" he said, like it was so hard to believe how charming I was.

"Yeah, I mean she didn't say it or anything, but I'm pretty sure that's because she didn't want to make the other kids jealous. But she couldn't stop looking at my handsome face." I raised my chin and posed like a model. Dad snorted.

"Gee, I wonder where he gets that healthy sense of self-esteem?" Mom said. I knew she was actually making fun of Dad because whenever he was in a bathing suit, he sucked in his stomach, flexed his arms like a bodybuilder, and said, "Mr. Universe has arrived, ladies. Try not to faint."

"What?" Dad said, acting like he had no idea

what she was talking about. "When you got it, you got it. The kid knows." He winked at me.

Mom rolled her eyes. "I got a text from Aunt Robin about the thank-you note you sent her," she said to me. "She thought it was very"—she paused for a second—"creative."

She held up her phone to show Dad. He read my note out loud:

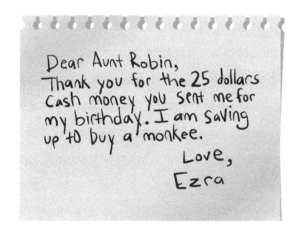

Dear Aunt Robin,
Thank you for the 25 dollars
Cash money you sent me for
my birthday. I am saving
up to buy a monkee.
            Love,
            Ezra

"You spelled *monkey* wrong," he told me.

Mom gave him a look. "Really? That's all you have to say about that?"

"We already have two kids and a barely

housebroken dog. What's the big deal about a monkey in the mix?"

Just then, the waitress came over to our table. "You folks ready to order?"

Before anyone could answer, I said, "Well, for my *birthday* dinner, I'll have the chicken nuggets with fries."

I needed to make sure she knew it was my birthday so that Elly the Elephant and all the people working there would come out to sing and I'd get a scoop of ice cream with a candle in it. I knew that almost-ten-year-olds were too old for it, but my friends weren't there, so I didn't care. Plus, when Elly and the servers sang to you, everyone in the entire restaurant turned around, and sometimes other tables started singing too, so everyone paid attention.

"Today is your birthday?" she asked.

"Yup," I said, even though it was only Thursday and my actual birthday wasn't for another three days. Luckily, no one said anything, not even Emmie.

"I'll have the chicken nuggets and fries too," she said. "I'm six," she added.

She looked at me, and I knew she was afraid I would tell the waitress she was only five—but if I did then she might say it wasn't my actual birthday, so I kept my mouth shut.

The waitress, who was about 106, looked up from her little notepad and smiled. "Oh, those beautiful blond curls. Aren't *you* a little Shirley Temple?" I had no idea who Shirley Temple was, but she must have been Emerson's twin because old ladies *always* said that.

It was (almost) *my* birthday, and as usual, my little sister was upstaging me. I crossed my arms and sat back in the booth. It didn't matter where we were. Every single time we went anywhere, adults always commented on how cute Emmie was. No one ever noticed me at all.

Mom and Dad ordered their meals, and the waitress left.

"So? How'd it go getting the phone?" asked Dad.

Mom was holding the bag with my birthday present. She'd wanted to wait until we were all together to "officially" give it to me.

I'd been waiting this whole year to get a phone. Mom and Dad had always said I couldn't get one until the fall when I was in middle school, and even though I told them when each of my friends got a phone and how I was going to be the only kid without one, they always said no. It wasn't until Zack—the one with the strictest mom of all—got a phone that they finally believed me.

"Happy birthday," she said as she started to hand me the bag. Before she let me take it, though, she said, "After tonight, no phones at the table." I nodded and grabbed it.

I used the table knife to open the cellophane wrapper, and when I pressed the button, it already had a little power. I could start using it right away! I had seen my friends take so many selfies that I already knew how, and I immediately started taking selfies and pictures of my family.

I didn't want to put the phone down, even when the food came. I picked up two fries and put them up my nose, one in each nostril.

"I'm a walrus," I said, taking another selfie. Emmie laughed.

"That's *disgusting*," snapped Mom. "Take those out of your nose this minute." I pulled them out of my nose and ate them, and she wasn't happy about that either. "Ezra!" she said in her really mad voice.

"Well," said Dad, "you told him to take them out. You didn't say, 'and don't eat them.'"

Emmie looked at her plate. Two of her nuggets were stuck together at the top. "Look," she said. "A heart." I could see that they also looked like something else. I took them out of her hands and turned them the other way.

"Or a butt," I said, taking another picture. I made it my screen saver, it was so good.

Dodgeballing

"Happy Birthday to youuuuuuuu," my best friend, Jasper, sang in a fake opera-singer voice when his nanny, Josephine, dropped him off at my birthday party at KidzGymtastic.

Dad gave Jasper a high five and said, "Hey, look, Ez, your twin is here." People always used to say that because Jasper and I both have dark brown curly hair and light brown eyes, and until this year we were almost exactly the same size. But Jasper's grown like six inches since last summer.

"Hi, Mr. Miller," Jasper said, then handed

me an envelope with a bow on it. "It's a gift card to the App Store. I'll show you the best games." I just nodded, though, since the rest of my friends were all arriving at the same time.

But before everyone was in the door, the guy in charge blew his whistle. "OK, friends! We are here to celebrate Ezra's birthday! Everybody, give him a round of applause!" Wow. I liked him already. "My name is Taylor. You can call me T. Who knows how to play dodgeball?" Everybody went wild. Everybody except Emmie, who did not want to play, which was good because I didn't want her to. She took her coloring book and lay down in the corner.

T blew his whistle again. "Ground rules: One. No hitting each other in the face, or you're out. That's it. You know the rest."

I heard Dad tell Mom, "He could have just said ground *rule*."

T had us count off *one-two*, which was kind of a bummer because if I'd known, I wouldn't have stood next to Jasper—I'd have stood next to Zack, who was the smallest by far and afraid of any ball in any sport, so he ran away from them. Dodgeball was probably the only time when that happened to be a pretty good quality, though, so it wasn't terrible.

Luckily, Matthew Rodef was on my team too. Even though he wasn't the biggest kid, he was strong and great at sports.

You really wanted Matthew on your side—because if he wasn't, it could be terrifying. When he got into a game, he sometimes forgot who his friends were, and he always wanted to win, so you could never play just for fun. But if you cared about winning, he was the best guy to have because he always played his hardest. Plus, he could whip a dodgeball like nobody's business. He once took out two people with a single throw when it ricocheted off the first person and then hit someone else. It was legendary.

We also had Henry, Jason, and Nelson on our team. Nelson was a good athlete, but he was also the tallest, which didn't help at all in dodgeball because, unlike Zack, he couldn't just make his body small and hard to hit. Owen, Danny, Josh, Lucas, Leo, and Jasper were on the other team. Jasper pointed at me and mouthed, "You're going down."

When the whistle blew, Matthew immediately hurled the ball so hard it whizzed past everyone on the other team, bounced off the wall, and hit Lucas in the back.

"Yer out," yelled Matthew.

"What?! No, I'm not. That ball was out before it was back in again, so it's a dead ball."

T blew his whistle and said that Lucas was right. Matthew looked mad, but he always gets a little mad whenever he doesn't win, even if it's just a single point.

After a couple of games, we went to the back room, where everyone sang "Happy Birthday" to me, and we had cake.

Then I got to open the presents. Mom wrote down who gave me what so I could send thank-you notes. I mostly got gift cards, but I also got a football, a Phillies cap, and a Junior Bug Collector kit that had a mini magnifying glass, plastic tweezers, and a plastic cup with a lid to collect bug "specimens." That was from Zack, of course. Zack gave the worst gifts, but it wasn't his fault; I knew it was his mom. I really had to pretend to like it. I deserved an Academy Award in the category of "Convincing People You Like an Educational Gift."

"No broken bones, no tears, and no damage we have to pay for," said Dad, after everyone had left. "By any measure, a complete success."

Emmie gave me a hopeful look and said, "If you don't want any of your presents, I'll take them."

"You can have this one." I handed her the bug collector kit. Then I turned to Mom. "Shouldn't Emmie have to write the thank-you note for that present if I'm letting her keep it?"

"Nice try," said Mom.

Chicken Butt

"Great party yesterday," Jasper said, sitting down next to me on the bus. He only lived three blocks away, and I always saved him a seat.

"Thanks," I said.

"What was the best present you got?"

"My grandparents got me a Sixers jersey, so that was pretty cool." He looked disappointed, so I said, "But yours was the best gift from any of my friends." It was clear he didn't really believe me. "I already used it to buy some games."

"Show me what games you got."

I wasn't sure if he said that because he was

suspicious or because he really wanted to see them. Either way, I pressed the button to get back to the home screen.

"What's that?" He pointed to my screen saver.

I explained about Emmie's chicken nuggets at Elly Fants and how they looked like a butt.

"Chicken butt!" Jasper said, laughing. "You gotta send it to me."

I did, and then, because he liked it so much, I posted it on my new Instagram account that Mom let me get when I told her that even Zack had an Instagram. I didn't mention that his mom let him get it so that he could post the covers of all the books he read. Under the photo I wrote the words "Chicken Butt."

Our bus always arrived at school at the same time as about five other buses. Mr. Brubaker, the principal, was standing in front of the sign that said "Sean Hughes Elementary School" when we got off, yelling at kids to keep moving and not block the path.

Mr. Brubaker wore a brown suit every single day, and today was no different, even though it was May and already about a million degrees out. His bald head was so sweaty that he looked like the plastic man from Emmie's Play-Doh kit when you put Play-Doh inside and push down and it squeezes out of a thousand holes at the top of the head like hair. Except that, instead of sticking out like Play-Doh, the sweat on top of Mr. Brubaker's head was just rolling down his forehead and neck, making his collar so wet that it was a darker color than the rest of his shirt. So gross.

Matthew jumped off the last step of his bus and ran to catch up to us. I looked over at Mr. Brubaker to see if he was going to yell at Matthew for running, but he was too busy yelling at a girl who had stopped to tie her shoe.

"Was that really a chicken's butt?" said Matthew.

"No," I said, "it was just two chicken nuggets stuck together." I was glad Matthew liked it because he made fun of people if they did dumb stuff.

"Duh," said Jasper, rolling his eyes. "Obviously it wasn't a real chicken's actual butt. A real chicken butt would have feathers on it."

Matthew glared at Jasper. "I know," he said. "I obviously meant, Was it real chicken nuggets?"

"Yeah," I said quickly. I was pretty sure Matthew didn't know it was nuggets, and even though he could dish it out, he didn't take it very well when someone else made fun of him, so I wanted to protect Jasper from getting pounded. "It was real nuggets that we got at Elly Fants. They came just like that."

By then we were all inside the fifth-grade hallway. Matthew, Nelson, and Jasper went into their homeroom. When I walked into Ms. Robinson's room, Zack, Danny, and Lucas were already in their seats. I put my phone in the front pocket of my backpack and zipped it up so I wouldn't lose it.

After attendance and the Pledge of

Allegiance, we had health class since it was Monday. Ms. Robinson left when our gym teacher, Mr. Volpi, walked in. I'm not really sure who chose him to be a gym teacher, or even to teach health, since he smelled like cigarettes all the time—even first thing in the morning.

Today he didn't even say hello, like usual. He just walked straight up to the blackboard and wrote one word and underlined it. Then he turned back to us so we could see what he'd written.

HYGIENE

"Hygiene," he said running his hands through his straggly hair. "Time to talk about what happens if you don't clean your bodies."

● ● ●

"Oh man, I thought it would never be lunch," Danny moaned as we walked into the cafeteria, over to where Zack was already in his usual seat at our usual table. "I've been starving since I got off the bus."

I couldn't believe it. "You've been starving since health? I thought I was going to barf thinking about whether Volpi showered." I was still queasy.

"Yeah," said Danny, shrugging. "I'm always starving."

Nelson put his lunch down and said, "That picture of the chicken butt was hilarious."

"I know, right?" Matthew dropped off his binder at his normal seat at the end. "When I saw it, I almost swallowed my gum."

Zack's eyes grew wide. "You're allowed to chew gum?" Zack, of course, was not allowed.

"Yeah."

"In the morning?" Zack seemed like he could not believe his ears.

"My mom doesn't care," Matthew said casually. "Plus, she didn't know I had a piece in my pocket when I left this morning."

"You're my hero." Zack began to arrange his usual weird lunch. First, he opened his re-usable lunch sack, took out a napkin, and then on top of it he put a whole-wheat wrap with what looked like avocado, bean sprouts, and some kind of lumpy cheese, a cheese stick, kale chips, and a peach.

When he noticed we were staring, he tried to stuff most of it back in the bag.

Matthew pulled a five-dollar bill out of his pocket. "My mom made my favorite," he said with a smile as he jogged over to the lunch line.

Jasper unzipped the front compartment of his backpack and found a plastic baggie with money in it. "Oh good, Josephine remem-bered." He followed Matthew.

"Anyone want to trade kale chips for potato chips?" Zack asked hopefully.

Dad had packed me three Oreos, but I wasn't very hungry. I pushed one over to Zack. "You can keep your kale chips."

He shoved the Oreo in his mouth as if he was worried I'd try to take it back.

"How many likes did your chicken butt picture get?" asked Zack.

I thought for a minute. "When I checked before the bell rang this morning, it already had twelve likes." Even though twelve likes weren't enough to seem popular, it was pretty good considering I had just posted it riding the bus.

"That's good," said Matthew as he and Jasper came back with their trays. "It was really funny. I bet by this afternoon you'll have more."

I was psyched, but before I could enjoy the excitement too much, Carter Williams came over. We all stopped talking.

Carter was the coolest kid at Hughes, and he knew it—and so did everyone else, including all the other guys chosen for travel soccer and all the mean, popular girls who giggled at everything he said and invited him to their parties.

"What time is the game on Saturday?" he asked Matthew, who was on the travel soccer team with him. He didn't bother even saying hi to anyone else at our table—didn't even look at us—even though he used to come over to my house to play when we were little. But that was a long time ago when our dads golfed together. Then his parents got divorced, and Mr. Williams moved to New York. Now, Carter pretended he didn't even know who I was.

Matthew sat with us during lunch, but the popular kids still talked to him because of travel soccer. He was even sometimes invited to their parties that weren't birthday parties. They were just parties where the travel soccer guys hung out with the popular girls.

Sounded boring to me, so I pretty much didn't care that I wasn't at those sit-around-and-hang-out kinds of parties . . . but it kind of bothered me that I never got asked. I would never have said that to him or anyone else though.

"Eight o'clock," answered Matthew.

"Ugh. So early." Carter shook his head as

he walked away. We all stayed quiet until he was gone.

Zack was the first one to break the silence. "Anyone want to trade anything for a delicious peach?" He held up the peach like he was on a game show.

That's when I noticed it looked just like a butt. I wanted that peach. But I'd already given him an Oreo and gained nothing in return. All I had left was a half-empty baggie of Cheez-Its.

"I'll trade you this for it." I pushed the bag over.

"Deal!" said Zack, grabbing it. He placed the first Cheez-It on his tongue and seemed to be letting it dissolve. He closed his eyes and smiled. I put the peach in the pocket of my shorts to save for later.

Peach Butt

Mom and Emmie were arguing in the kitchen when I got home. For once, Mom wasn't agreeing with her or taking her side like she always did whenever I was arguing with Emmie.

"Why can't you?" Emmie whined. I had already taken my phone out of my backpack, so I just dumped the backpack on the floor, checked that I still had the peach in my pocket, and tried to run upstairs while Mom wasn't paying attention.

"Wait one minute!" she yelled up at me. "Come back downstairs and do your homework before you go to your room."

I sighed as I came back down. "Can I at least have a snack first?"

"Fine," said Mom, giving me a box of sourdough pretzels. She turned to get some milk from the refrigerator.

Emmie wouldn't let whatever it was go. "Why can't you?" she asked. Of course, she didn't notice or care that Mom was busy getting my snack.

"You know why I can't. I work during the day. Besides, I went on the last field trip. It wouldn't be fair to the other parents who haven't gotten a chance to go on one yet."

"But this is a trip to the *Insectarium*," Emmie moaned, as if that was somehow going to convince Mom.

"I'll try to go on the next one." Mom set a glass of milk in front of me.

"But this is the last field trip of the year. I don't even know if they have field trips in first grade."

"They do. I promise I'll go on the very first one of the year, Emmie."

My sister crossed her arms and huffed, "Don't call me Emmie anymore."

"OK," said Mom patiently. "What should I call you?"

I figured she'd say, "Call me Emerson," but instead she said, "You can call me Princess Cupcake Dingleberry."

I laughed, then choked, and milk shot out of my nose and mouth. Mom rushed over with a paper towel.

"How was your day?" she asked me after I was OK.

"Fine."

"What did you do at school?"

"Nothing."

She smiled and shook her head. "OK, good talk. Do your homework."

I didn't want to *do* my homework, but I wanted to be *done* with my homework so I could go upstairs to get a picture of the peach. Instead of arguing, I unzipped my backpack and fished out my boring social studies packet about freedom of speech. As I was finishing the last question about whether schools could suspend a student for a Facebook post, Mom's phone rang. I could tell by her tone that it was someone from her office, so I finished and ran upstairs before she hung up.

Whenever our dog, Lucy, saw anyone running, she would assume something exciting was happening, so she would start running too. Now she jumped up from where she'd been lying under the kitchen table and raced after me.

I closed the door when I got to my room, but Lucy started scratching to be let in. As soon as I did, she realized nothing was happening and flopped down on the floor. I shut the door quietly behind her.

It took a couple of tries to get the picture of the peach so it looked like a butt but didn't have my shadow over it. I finally got it just right. So right that it really, really looked like a butt.

I captioned it "Peach Butt!" and posted it.

The likes started rolling in almost right away.

Five minutes later, I got an alert: "Carter Williams has started following you." My heart skipped a beat.

Within ten minutes, six other people started following me, and one of them was Carter's best friend, Alex Robertson.

The year before, I had signed up to run for school treasurer before I knew that Alex was running too. He gave out chocolate coins as if that proved he would be a good treasurer, even though giving out anything was against the rules. But he didn't get disqualified, and of course, he won. Not because of the chocolate and not because of his math skills (I was in a higher math class than he was).

He won because he was a popular kid, and as it turned out, being popular was even more important than whether you actually deserved it.

But at that moment, I didn't care about losing to Alex; I was so happy that he and Carter were following me. Maybe they'd stop by our table to talk to me instead of Matthew.

One of my new followers was from Little League. Two others were girls in my class. I didn't recognize the names of the rest, who used animals for their profile pictures, but maybe they were friends with Carter and Alex? Didn't know, didn't care.

All I knew was that I was going to be as popular as Carter Williams—maybe even *more* popular—and he and his friends wouldn't treat me as if I were invisible anymore, all because of my funny posts.

I picked up the peach and took a bite. Looks were deceiving. It was so hard that it hurt my front teeth. The trade was still definitely worth it though.

Partners

The second I got off the bus at school the next day, Zack was there. I was pretty sure he'd been waiting for me.

"Was that the peach I gave you?" he asked. "The one you used in your peach butt picture?" It was like he was somehow trying to take credit, although I didn't really care because that meant he liked it.

"Yeah," I said.

It was obvious he had never been so excited about having fruit instead of a real dessert. "I thought so. I told my mom to pack me another peach, but I didn't tell her why," he said, like we were in on a secret together. "But the one she packed today is rounder than yesterday's, so it doesn't really look as much like a butt. But you could still use it."

"Nah, that would be boring," said Matthew, who joined the conversation as he caught up with us. "He's got to do something totally different."

"Totally different?" Jasper had joined us, and his voice had a little edge on it—as usual, he was getting into it a little with Matthew. It didn't take much to set them off. For example, Matthew was a Giants fan; whenever they won, he couldn't stop talking about how great they were compared to the Eagles, who Jasper loved. Usually Danny said something funny to stop them from arguing, but he wasn't there.

"How could they be totally different?" Jasper asked a second time. "He's only posting pictures of things that look like butts."

I was psyched when he said that. I felt like I was getting known for something.

Matthew rolled his eyes. "I know they're all butts, *Jasper*." He put the emphasis on the name "Jasper" so everyone would know he thought Jasper's comment was dumb. Matthew was the first one to get TikTok and Instagram— before anyone else even had a phone—so he was the expert. "But they have to be different *kinds* of butts, or they'll get boring and people will stop caring. You can't repeat butt types," he said in a serious tone, nodding at me.

Good advice. I nodded back.

I was still curious about the people who'd started following me yesterday. "Who's Sophisti-Cat? I don't know who that is, and the picture is of a cat, so I can't tell."

"That's Sophie Bodinny," said Matthew. "She followed you?"

"Yeah."

Sophie had her appendix out in first grade and missed so much school that she repeated the year, which was why she was a full head taller than most of the boys. The popular kids used to tease her because she was so tall and skinny, but this year she'd grown out her hair and gotten contacts, and they'd started to invite her to their parties.

"Skinny Bodinny is following you?" asked Zack, using her old nickname.

"She's not skinny in some places anymore," said Matthew, rubbing his chest to show where she wasn't skinny anymore and smiling. "I heard she wears a bra." Zack turned red. I pretended I didn't notice.

Seriously, who cared about Sophie?

"Yeah, I guess she heard about my posts from Carter." I tried to sound casual.

Jasper's eyes grew wide. "Carter Williams followed you?"

"No way," said Zack.

Matthew either didn't hear, didn't care, or was still thinking about Sophie.

Me, I did my best not to smile.

I wanted to see if I had any new followers, but the bell rang before I could check, and I had to put my phone in my backpack. I definitely did not want Ms. Robinson to take it away.

After attendance and the Pledge, I expected Senorita Goldberg to come in since we usually had Spanish first on Tuesdays. Ms. Robinson saw us looking at the door and said, "We're not having Spanish right now, class. We need to go to the auditorium for graduation practice."

Everyone started talking at once. A few kids clapped.

"Settle down or you're not going!" Ms. Robinson yelled. She's usually pretty soft-spoken, but when she yells, you can hear her over a stampede.

In the sudden quiet, she cleared her throat. "Thank you," she said. "Line up in two single-file lines, boys in one and girls in the other."

She didn't need to tell us twice. Usually, she told us it was *not* time to line up at the door, like when we still had five minutes of school left, but this time she was telling us to line up when we had been at school for only five minutes in the first place.

We marched down the hall in two lines. When we got to the auditorium, we walked down the center aisle, and she had the boys turn right and the girls turn left as we filed into rows behind kids from the other classes.

"OK, ladies and gentlemen," Mr. Brubaker said when he took the stage. Nobody even noticed; we were all still talking to each other. He put two fingers in his mouth and whistled so loudly everyone stopped dead. Zack, who was two seats away from me, covered his ears.

"Nobody's going to Dorney Park if you don't quiet down." We shut up right away. The fifth-grade graduation trip to Dorney Park and Wildwater Kingdom amusement park was legendary. We'd all been looking forward to it since first grade.

"You will walk down the aisle in pairs—one boy, one girl. When you get to the front, boys will turn right, go up the steps on the right side of the stage, and fill up the rows of chairs on the right side, starting in the back. When you fill up the back row, you'll go to the next row until you get to the front. Girls, same thing except on the left side. If someone isn't here today, leave a space for that person so we'll have the correct lineup at graduation."

Zack let out a whoop. "Ha! Take that, Abhishek Abdi." Abhishek, who was sitting two rows in front of Zack, jumped a little.

Abhishek turned around. "What?"

"You're first whenever we line up in alphabetical order, by first name *or* by last name. But this time, even though you're going to get called first, you'll be in back, and I'll be in front."

This was obviously a big deal for a kid named Zack Zucker, who only got to be first when we lined up in size order, which he hated.

I waited until Mr. Brubaker called my name. Not as long as Zack would have to wait, of course, but it took a long time even to get to the middle of the alphabet. "Ezra Miller, Lilly Mensh," he finally said.

I was psyched. Lilly was about the best I could have for a girl partner. Our moms met in college, so we had known each other since we were born. Some years, the two of us were in the same class. This year, Lilly had Ms. Hirsh for homeroom with Matthew and Jasper, but we were ranked by ability in math, so she and I were together in the highest math class.

I liked that she was smart because she always helped me if I didn't quite understand the homework—or had forgotten to do it, which I sometimes did, but she never did—and she was pretty cool. Not cool in the unlikable way the popular girls were cool, but cool because she laughed at my jokes and didn't seem to care that the popular girls ignored her. I was glad that she smiled when I stood next to her.

Jasper was the next boy called, which I was also happy about, even though I knew he'd be right behind me because his last name was Moray. Unfortunately for Jasper, he got paired up with Molly Murtaugh, who was about half a foot taller than he was and could probably pound him into the ground. Judging by the mad look that was always on her face, it kind of seemed like she wanted to. I could not understand why she was popular, since the other popular girls were mostly mean by ignoring kids who weren't like them. But Molly was a bully.

This made me even happier to be paired up with Lilly. I could tell that Jasper was jealous.

We marched down the aisle together, and then we separated at the steps as we walked up to the stage. I took my seat on the aisle, and the kids kept coming. When my friends passed me, they slapped me on the shoulder or gave me a high five.

Then Carter Williams passed by, turned around, and looked me right in the eye. "Hey," he said with a nod.

"Hey," I said, nodding back without smiling,

as if getting acknowledged by him was no big deal. I really hoped my friends noticed.

Things were turning out awesome now that I had my phone.

Once everyone was seated, Mr. Brubaker started talking about boring stuff like how we would all turn to face the flag when we said the Pledge and who was going to speak, blah, blah, blah. If I had my phone, I could have been texting my friends or playing Mario Kart.

I sat there just staring at my hands while Mr. Brubaker yammered on and on. I made a fist with my thumb tucked in, and that's when I noticed it.

Right where my thumb met the rest of my hand, it made a line that looked like a butt! Another butt! Everywhere I looked, I could find a butt. I was getting great at this.

I would definitely take a picture as soon as I got home.

Free Samples

"How many times have I told you to turn off the TV?" Mom yelled. I couldn't say, exactly. I wasn't really paying attention.

In my defense, I was busy. I was watching TV at the same time I was checking to see how many new followers I'd gotten from my latest butt picture. It wasn't perfect—you could kind of see the other wrinkles on my hand, so you could tell it wasn't an actual butt. Still, new followers were rolling in.

Anyway, I wasn't happy to be dragged off to the mall on a sunny Memorial Day to go shopping with Mom and Emmie; I was perfectly happy in the basement, watching TV and playing on my phone.

It wasn't that I hated all shopping. I mean, sports equipment was a great thing to buy. Sneakers, Halloween costumes, toys—all errands I didn't mind doing. I didn't even hate grocery shopping because I could usually convince Mom to buy good cereal, versus if I wasn't there, she'd come back with some "healthy" brand in a box the color of brown cardboard. (Which, by the way, was usually what the cereal inside the box tasted like.)

But buying khaki pants for my graduation? The ones I had were fine. Mom said that they were two inches too short and made me look like a castaway, which I thought was kind of cool, actually. I asked her to just pick out any pair, but she made me come along. Something about them needing to fit.

I tried on five different pairs of pants, and she almost made me try on two of them again so she could "compare."

"It doesn't matter what pair. They're all khaki," I muttered—although, when I thought about it, there was one pair that was a little more brownish. "Except that one, which is the color of barf. Just pick one. I don't care. Except not the barf one."

Mom shrugged. "Fine," she said. "These will be fine." She held them up. "I'll pay, and then I just need to go to the makeup counter to get my moisturizer, and then we can go home."

Aaaarrrgh. *Another* stop before we got home. She could see how I felt, so she said, "The longer you spend arguing, the longer it'll take to get out of here. This will only be a minute."

"Yay!" said Emmie. "Maybe they'll give you free samples?"

"If you behave while we're there and they give me samples, you can have them."

"Yay!" Emmie said again as Mom paid for the pants.

Of course, there was a line at the makeup counter.

I couldn't believe how many people were at the mall. A perfectly sunny day—a *holiday*—and even people who didn't need khaki pants were shopping on purpose. Seriously, what was wrong with them?

Mom was in line behind a woman who was letting the counter lady put different eye shadows on her. Emmie disappeared around the other side of the counter, where they had the perfumes.

She was picking up glass bottles from a tray, and when she saw me she held out one that was in the shape of an apple, even though she knew she wasn't supposed to touch anything. But, as always, she wouldn't get in trouble because she was "*so* cute."

I smelled it. It just smelled like perfume.

She put it down, picked up another one, and tried it. "This one's like roses," she said, and then looked over at Mom, who was busy talking to the counter lady. Emmie squirted it on her wrist and held it up for me to smell.

Yuck. I wrinkled my nose. "Too flowery," I said. I knew if anyone saw us, I could blame my sister because it was her idea, so I picked up a different bottle. It smelled like orange peels.

"Try this one," I said. She held out her other wrist.

Now it was her turn to wrinkle her nose. "Too spicy."

We both started picking up and smelling all the different perfumes. When Emmie found ones she liked, she squirted them on different parts of her arm.

The next one I took must have been the perfume my teacher wore because it smelled just like her. Weird! "I think this is Ms. Robinson's perfume."

"I like it. Spray it here," she said, pointing to the inside of her elbow.

I had an idea. "OK, don't look. I'll spray you with one, and you decide if you like it or not."

Emmie thought this was great. She bent her arm and put her head down so she couldn't see what I was doing. I looked back over at her and noticed that the inside of her bent arm looked like a butt crack. It was like everywhere I looked I could find something butt-like!

I tried to get out my phone, but I had a bottle of perfume in my hand. "Are you going to spray me or not?" Emmie said a little loudly. I was afraid Mom would hear, so I stopped and just sprayed the next bottle. "I can't really smell it. They're all kind of blending together." Then she said, "Oh, wait!" She lifted the bottom of her shirt. "My tummy."

When the mist from the perfume hit her stomach, she giggled. I checked, and Mom was handing the counter lady a credit card, so we were almost done.

Just as I was about to spray Emmie's knee-cap, Mom called, "Let's go, guys. I'm all finished here."

We ducked back into the aisle as if nothing had happened and ran ahead of her to the car.

When we got near the car, Mom pulled

out the key fob so she could unlock the doors from a few feet away. Emmie climbed into her booster seat, and I got in next to her.

It smelled like an explosion in a perfume factory. I started breathing through my mouth.

Mom leaned in to get to Emmie's seat belt. For a second, she looked confused, and then I could tell she realized Emmie was wearing a lot of perfume.

At that exact minute, the smell must have gotten to Emmie too because she sneezed so hard that the hair on the side of Mom's head blew back like it was caught in the wind. Gross! Mom's ear was wet from the sneeze too, and she pulled back, trying to wipe it off.

"What did you *do*?" she asked, a little horrified. I braced myself.

"I sneezed. You're supposed to say, 'God bless you,'" Emmie said, sounding offended.

"God *bless* you?" Mom said in disbelief.

"Thank you," replied Emmie.

"How many perfumes did you try on?" Mom

asked, now that it was clear why we'd been so quiet while she was buying moisturizer.

"Well, three on this hand." Emmie held up her right arm. I had to give it to my sister: she either wasn't scared that she was going to get in trouble or didn't think we'd done anything wrong. I figured it was best to let her handle this. "And maybe two on this arm, and one on my tummy, and one on—"

Before she could finish, she drew in a deep breath. Another earthshaking sneeze was coming.

This time Mom knew what was about to happen. Without another word she closed Emmie's door, waited for her to sneeze, then got in the front seat, turned on the car, opened all the windows, and backed out of the parking spot.

"You're going into the tub the second we get home, Emmie."

Whew. Even though Mom still seemed mad, she said "Emmie" instead of "Emerson Anne Miller," which was what she called her when she was really, really mad, although that was pretty rare. Like I said, Emmie almost never got in trouble.

We drove all the way home with the windows open, which we didn't usually do when we were on the highway because it was so noisy. I was glad for the noise, though, because it meant Mom couldn't really say anything else.

When we pulled into the garage, I moved fast so I could get to my room and take an elbow butt pic. Before I closed the car door, I heard Emmie ask Mom, "Did you get any free samples that I can have?" Mom just sighed.

My Hypothesis

I had my hand on the garage doorknob when Mom called out, "Wait! Take your pants with you." She handed me the bag. I ran into the house, but not before I heard her add, "Hang them up and then come right down. Dad already has dinner on the table."

I threw the bag into my closet.

Yes, I did really want to take that elbow butt picture, but dinner smelled great and I was starving. Everyone else was in the kitchen. Dad was standing at the sink with his back to the table, but I saw him turn around and sniff the air. "Lisa, did you get a new perfume?"

"No," said Mom. "Our daughter thought she should try on every single perfume in the store when I wasn't looking."

I knew she was scolding Emmie, but again, Emmie didn't get it. "Don't I smell like a grown-up lady, Daddy?" she asked with a big smile. For once, I wasn't mad when I saw Dad's "she *is* very cute" look because Emmie hadn't said a word about my part, which I appreciated. I hoped they'd just drop it.

They did. "Who did something fun today?" asked Dad, like always.

"I did!" said Emmie.

"Yes," he replied with a smile. "So I gathered."

Mom spoke up. "Before I forget, Ezra, did you get the tickets for graduation? I want to mail them off to Nana and Pop tomorrow."

"Oh, yeah," I said. My backpack was under her desk in the kitchen where I'd dropped it the minute I got home from school on Friday. "Ms.

Robinson said we can have more if we need them." I opened the "Take Home" folder where I had put them.

That was when I saw the reminder assignment sheet that Ms. Robinson had given us three weeks earlier. My heart dropped into my stomach.

I handed Mom the tickets and asked casually, "Uh, what's tomorrow's date?"

"May twenty-ninth," said Dad. "Why?"

"Do we have any poster board?"

"You can check the back closet after dinner. We probably have a piece or two left," said Mom. Even though I was doing my best to make it seem like a totally normal conversation, she was suspicious. "Why are you asking, Ezra?" I didn't say anything. I knew I was caught. "What's due tomorrow that you're just starting to think about now?"

"Nothing," I muttered. "Just some stupid project for science."

"What project?" asked Dad.

"A stupid project for the fifth-grade science fair. But it's not a big deal."

"Wait," said Mom. "This isn't the project Ms. Robinson talked about in September when the parents came to Back-to-School Night, is it? The one that's the biggest project of fifth grade?"

"Um, yeah. I guess. But I'm mostly done."

"Mostly done how?" she asked. Man, she would not let up.

"Well, I've already picked a topic."

"That's it?" Her voice got loud. "All you've done is picked a topic? And it's due tomorrow?"

I hadn't actually picked a topic.

So, of course, she had to ask, "What's your topic?"

"Well . . ." I said slowly, stalling so I could come up with a topic—any topic. I looked around the kitchen and saw underneath the cabinet, where the cookbooks were, the pink bouncy ball I'd lost two weeks ago. "Well," I went on, "I want to see which ball bounces the high-est when it's dropped from the second-floor window. I *hypothesize* that the bouncy ball will bounce the highest."

Hypothesize is a word Ms. Robinson used all the time in science class. I was pretty impressed with myself, and I hoped Mom would be impressed too. Or at least be convinced that I had been working on the project all along.

She didn't seem impressed or convinced. "Dad's the scientist in the family. He can help you."

Dad looked up from the stove, blinking in surprise. Clearly, he was about as happy as I was at the turn this conversation had just taken.

"What?" he said. "How do you figure that being a human resources director makes me a scientist?"

"You're the one who fixes the printer when it stops working. And you took psychology in college, didn't you? That's science. Besides, I need to give *this* one"—she gestured toward Emmie—"a bath as soon as dinner is over, before my nose falls off. You win the science fair project."

"Fine," Dad grumbled, even though it didn't really sound like it was fine with him.

"I already have most of it figured out," I put in. "And anyway, I'm OK. When Emmie is out of the bath, she can help me." Whenever I included Emmie in anything, it made Mom and Dad happy, so I figured it would be a good idea.

We raced through dinner. Afterward, Mom and Emmie went upstairs. Dad went into the family room and turned on the Phillies game. I set off for the basement to get a ping-pong ball and find the tennis ball we threw for Lucy when we went to the park.

It took a while, but I found both of them and went up to my room to wait for Emmie. My phone buzzed, and I saw that Jasper had texted me.

JASPER:

My parents said I

might be having a

graduation party

ME:

Cool

What are u doin there

JASPER:

I don't know

They said I can have

people over

ME:

Thats cool whos

comin

JASPER:

YOU

ME:

Is anyone else

JASPER:

Maybe Lilly

ME:

LILLY

SHES A GIRL

JASPER:

Shes cool tho

ME:

🔫

SHES LITERALLY A

GIRL!!!!!

I could see that Jasper was typing, but just then Emmie ran into my room wearing her pj's. Her hair was brushed but still wet, and she didn't smell like anything anymore except shampoo.

"Ready to help!" she said, bouncing a little.

I stuck my phone in my pocket and opened my window. It faced onto the driveway, but the sloped garage roof was right below. I needed a straight drop. I couldn't use Emmie's windows because they were babyproofed. And no way was I going into Mom and Dad's room, where Mom might still be. I definitely did not want to see her until I'd finished. My window over the garage would have to do.

"OK," I told Emmie, "I'm going to test my hypothesis." It did sound kind of scientific. I opened the window and pushed up the screen.

"You stay here," I said. "I'll go down to the driveway, and when I tell you to, throw each ball down so I can see which bounces highest and record it. But you have to throw it hard— kind of over and down, so it goes over the top of the garage and bounces on the driveway."

We looked out the window together.

"Oh," I added, "and you should probably keep both of your feet on the floor when you throw the balls out the window. If you fall out, Mom and Dad will kill me."

"OK," she said happily.

I handed her the balls, then ran down the steps and out the door. Lucy thought something exciting must be going on, so she followed me outside and flopped on the grass next to the driveway.

I could feel my phone buzzing in my pocket. More texts.

JASPER:

Can u ask her for me

You talk to her

                              ME:

                               Y

JASPER:

Shes cool

She talks to both of us

                               ME:

                         Then u ask her

JASPER:

BRO!!!!

SHES A GIRL

Before I could think of a response, I heard Emmie yelling.

"What should I do now?"

"OK, when I say, 'Go,' throw the ping-pong ball," I yelled back. "On your mark, get set . . ." I put my thumb on my screen, flicked out of texting, opened the camera app, and held up the phone. "Go!"

Emmie threw the ping-pong ball out the window. She got the "throw it over" part—it cleared the garage overhang—but not the "and down" part so much. It flew behind me, so even though I had the slo-mo video on, I didn't get the bounce because it was behind me when it hit the driveway.

Then it started to roll down toward the street. I started after it, but it reached the street just as a car was driving past, and the ball was squashed flat.

"Why did you throw it so hard?" I yelled up to Emmie. "Now it's ruined!"

"Sorry! I promise, promise, *promise* I won't do it so hard the next time."

Of course I was mad, but there was nothing I could do. I'd have to find another ping-pong ball later, if we even had one. Plus, it was starting to get a little dark, so I figured we should just use what we had.

As I decided to delete the last video and try again with the tennis ball, my phone buzzed again.

> **JASPER:**
>
> Can u??

> **ME:**
>
> What?

> **JASPER:**
>
> Ask Lilly??

> **ME:**
>
> U like her u ask her
>
> Its ur girlfriend

He was typing again, but I had to stop texting so I could get this done already.

I yelled toward the window, "When I say go, this time throw it mostly downward. On your mark, get set, *go!*"

The tennis ball fell straight down, bounced off the garage overhang, and ricocheted sideways onto the grass, just a few feet from Lucy. Before I could reach it, she picked up the ball in her mouth and crawled under the bush in the corner of the yard.

I tried to grab it out of her mouth, but I tripped over a root and face-planted. My phone went flying, and I wound up covered in mud and grass.

"*Aaahhh!*" I punched the ground. "This is the worst!" And now my hand hurt too.

Dad came outside. He must have heard me yelling over the Phillies game. "What's up?" he asked, as if it wasn't obvious.

"This stinks," I groaned. I threw my head back and looked up at the sky, which had turned from light blue to dark blue because the sun was setting.

"Whoa, take it easy," Dad said. "Seems like this isn't the best way to test the bounce. Grab your phone, and let's head inside." I wiped my hands on my shorts. "Maybe wash off first," he added.

He looked up at my bedroom window. "Emmie, hold your fire." She made a thumbs-up sign. He called over toward the bush where Lucy was hiding. "Luuuuucy—c'mon, girl." Lucy appeared with half the tennis ball in her mouth.

"Oh, man," I said. I hated this stupid project, and I hated that I had waited until the last minute, and there was absolutely nothing I could do about it.

"It's OK," Dad told me. "I guess we'll cross 'tennis ball' off the list. What other balls do you have?"

I remembered that I'd left my basketball at Jasper's the last time we'd played, which made me even angrier. "We still have the bouncy ball, and I can get a football and a baseball from the garage, I guess. But it's so obvious that a football and a baseball won't bounce as high as a bouncy ball."

"You mean you *hypothesize* that the football

and the baseball won't bounce as high?" Dad winked at me.

I knew he was trying to be nice, but this really did stink. "I guess so." I was going to have the worst project in the whole science fair.

Meanwhile, my phone was buzzing up a storm.

JASPER:

BRO

BRO??

SHES A GIRL

ME:

wdtm

JASPER:

BRO

I can't ask her

ME:

Y

When we got inside, Dad said, "I have an idea. Why don't you have Emmie stand at the top of the steps and drop balls over the banister, while you record how high they bounce on the entry hall floor. No cars, and you don't have to worry that it's too dark."

Emmie was so happy she still got to help that she went to the garage to find the baseball and football. That was nice of her, actually—although her bad throws were the reason I was in this mess. That, and not starting the project earlier. But mostly her bad throws.

We all got into position—Emmie at the top of the steps, Dad and I in the entry hall. I brushed the grass off my phone and turned on the video.

"Ready?" Dad asked me.

"Ready," I said.

He looked up at Emmie. "Ready, Emmie?"

"Ready, Freddie!" She held the football over the banister.

"OK, drop it."

I touched record. The football hit the floor,

took a sharp bounce to the side, grazed a vase of flowers on the entry hall table, and almost knocked it over. We all froze for a second until it stopped wobbling.

Dad was checking the video over my shoulder. Looked good—the first thing that had gone right so far. I was pretty sure he had seen Jasper's texts, so I quickly swiped up to hide them.

"It looks like it bounced back up to the third step," I said, relieved I could see it in slo-mo. I screenshotted how high the ball got. Whew.

Then Dad had to ruin it. "And how high is that?"

"What? I don't know. How high is each step?"

"Go get a ruler and find out." *Ugh.* This was so stupid. I went to the kitchen to find the ruler, but, of course, it wasn't in the drawer where it belonged.

"Where's the ruler?" I yelled.

"Where did you leave it the last time you used it?"

I banged the drawer shut. "I have no idea. If I knew where it was, I wouldn't be asking!"

Dad didn't say another word. He left the room, went into the garage, and came back with the measuring tape from his toolbox. Together, we measured the step. It was eight inches.

"So eight times three equals twenty-four inches to the third step," I said.

"Great," said Dad. "Write that down."

OMG, this project would never end! I stomped into the kitchen so he'd know I was mad about that too. I got a pencil and a piece of paper from my backpack and wrote down:

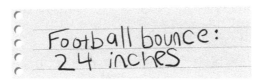

Football bounce:
24 inches

Jasper kept texting, and Dad looked at me every time my phone buzzed. I ignored him.

He raised his voice. "OK, Emmie, grab the baseball. Ezra, stop texting and record the bounce."

"I'm not texting." Which was true. Jasper was texting *me*.

Emmie dropped the baseball. It hit the floor with a huge thud, and Lucy ran away into the kitchen. I checked my phone. "I got the bounce. It only went up to the second step." I wrote down:

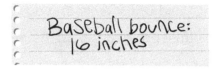

Baseball bounce: 16 inches

"And now, finally, the bouncy ball," said Dad.

Emmie and I were in position. She dropped it when Dad said, "Go," and it went all the way up to the eighth step.

"How high?" asked Dad after I checked my video.

"Eight times eight. Sixty-four inches."

"OK," Dad said as I wrote it down.

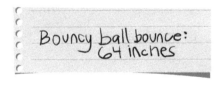

Bouncy ball bounce: 64 inches

"Great. Get the poster board and some markers, and you can get this baby done."

But when I went to the back closet, only one piece of poster board was left—it was hot pink and one corner was bent.

"Dad! What am I going to do?" I asked, panicked.

He looked up at the clock. "8:45 p.m. on Memorial Day? Nothing's open. You'll just have to make do."

I hung my head, but there was nothing I could say. And I didn't need to hear him tell me for the millionth time not to wait until the last minute.

"OK, Emmie—you were a great helper," he told my sister.

"Yeah," I added, because I knew I had to. "You were." She beamed.

While she went off to tell Mom she was ready for bed, I looked at what Jasper had texted.

JASPER:

I just can't talk to her

So will you do it

BRO

H

E

L

L

O

Where are u

ME:

doin my science

project

JASPER:

BRO

It's due tomorrow

I didn't have time to respond because Dad started yelling.

"Ezra, now is *not* the time to be texting your friends. If you didn't need those pictures to finish the project, I'd take that phone away. *Focus*."

He started rummaging through the desk. "I know that ruler is around here somewhere. We need to put down some lines so your writing will be straight—"

"No." I cut him off. "That'll take forever. It'll be fine." I could see he wanted to argue with me, but then he stopped himself, looked up at the clock, and took a deep breath.

I got the folder from my backpack and read the rules of the project. First, I had to write the question we *scientists* were going to answer. I wrote:

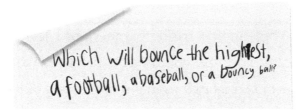

Which will bounce the highlest, a football, a baseball, or a bouncy ball?

Except I accidentally spelled *highest* with a *t* in the middle—*hightest*—but since it was in Sharpie, I couldn't erase it, so I had to cross out the *t* in the middle. Also, I realized a little too late that I had made the first couple of letters too big and I was going to run out of room, so I started making the letters smaller toward the end of the line. It was a little sloped, so it looked as if the question was climbing a hill. I looked over at Dad. He didn't say anything.

Next, the hypothesis. Below the question I wrote:

Hypothesis: I hypothesize that the bouncy ball will bounce the highest

This time, I tried to make the letters smaller so they would all fit, but they were too small, so I had to make the letters at the end bigger. Dad didn't say anything about that either.

Then I had to describe the experiment.

The experiment: I dropped a bouncy ball from the top of the steps to see which would bounce the highest.

I didn't even bother trying to fit it all on one line. I scrolled through the videos to the second you could see how high the balls bounced and sent the stills to the printer. I glued the pictures on the poster board with a glue stick and wrote how many inches each ball bounced under-neath.

Then, at the bottom, I wrote:

Conclusion: The bouncy ball bounced the highest

We looked at the finished poster. "I could draw a few random lines around the edges and rip it at the corners and call it art or something?" Maybe that would make it look better.

"No. Looks great. Time for bed," said Dad.

We both knew that it most definitely did not look great.

8

Tons of New Followers

As soon as I got to my room, I texted Jasper,
although I ignored his remark about not doing
my science fair project sooner.

ME:

Shes gonna think I
like her

JASPER:

Just tell her it's my party
Can u???

> **ME:**
>
> **fine**
>
> 😕

Since Jasper was my best friend, I texted Lilly even though I thought it was dumb.

> **ME:**
>
> **Jasper wants to know if u wanna go to his graduation party**

It was already after 9:00 p.m., and I didn't know if she was looking at her phone.

Then I remembered my elbow butt idea from the mall. I bent my elbow just like Emmie had, but instead of putting my head down on my arm, I moved my head away so that I could get a close-up.

It was butt-tastic! I was getting ready to post it when Jasper texted.

JASPER:

Did she write back yet

ME:

No

I started to go back to the elbow picture, but then my phone buzzed again.

LILLY:

does he like me?

jk

ME:

Idk maybe

LILLY:

lol

when is it

I didn't know what to say. I mean, yeah, he liked her. But I was starting to think he *liked her*, liked her, which was so weird because—what was he going to do? Go on dates with her?

Jasper and I always made fun of the popular boys who thought they were so cool telling everyone they went out with a girl, and all the popular girls who were so in love with Carter they'd turn red when he talked to them. Jasper used to say, "Oh, Carter, you're so handsome!" in a high-pitched voice and make kissing noises, and we'd crack up.

Now maybe he wanted to do that with Lilly? He'd be totally embarrassed if I told her.

ME:

I'll ask him when it is

A few moments later, she said:

LILLY:

If he lets me know I

can ask my mom

ME:

Aight

I really wanted to be done with this, so I thought about not telling Jasper, but I figured he'd bug me again if I didn't.

ME:

So Lilly wanted to know if u like her

JASPER:

😳

Did u tell her???

ME:

Possibly 😊

JASPER:

NO

BRO

ME:

HAHA U JUST GOT PLAYED

She said tell her when it is

so she can ask her mom

He was texting back, but I was done with this conversation.

I looked at my elbow butt picture, and it was great. I posted it with the caption: "Guess what part of my body this is?"

In minutes my phone began buzzing with likes, comments, and new followers.

DANNY: Is that really your butt?

SOPHIE: OMG

LILLY: Don't let your mom see this!

Jasper didn't respond to the picture, but he texted again.

JASPER:

Do you think she likes me?

I ignored that one.

Carter gave it three thumbs-up emojis. More likes started rolling in.

MATTHEW: 😂

I got a bunch of new followers, and more people were commenting and sending laughing emojis. I was so busy I didn't hear Mom until she came into my room.

"Ezra, it's past your bedtime. I thought Dad would have told you to go to bed." I heard the Phillies game from downstairs, which he must have turned on again once we were finished with the science project. "Put on your pj's and turn off your phone *now*."

I got my pajamas from my dresser, and then I just looked at her. She got the hint.

"I'll wait out in the hall. Don't dawdle."

I could hear my phone buzzing. I quickly changed, then plugged in the phone, and put it facedown on the dresser across the room. Then

I got into bed. "OK, you can come in," I said loudly.

Of course, she checked that the phone was charging and nowhere near me. Then she came over and kissed me on the forehead.

"Good night, Ez," she said, and turned off the light as she left.

"Good night," I replied. I waited to hear her go downstairs. Once she did, I quietly crossed the room, unplugged the phone, and brought it with me back to bed.

I had a couple of more notifications that people were following me and a few more comments.

ZACK: You shouldn't post this

Hilarious. They really thought it was my butt!

I bent my arm again but this time zoomed out so you could see my whole arm. It was dark, so I had to turn the flash on. I was praying Mom and Dad didn't walk by when I took the picture.

They didn't, luckily. I posted it.

> **ME:** 😆 It was my arm!

As soon as I sent it, I got a bunch of comments.

> **ZACK:** Haha. Very funny.
>
> **DANNY:** ROFL
>
> **LILLY:** Good
>
> **MATTHEW:** 😛
>
> **ALEX:** LOL
>
> **CARTER:** Good one

I heard the TV downstairs, the light-up Liberty Bell at Citizens Bank Park making the *Gong! Gong! Gong!* sound, which meant the game was over and the Phillies had won.

I felt like I'd won, too, with all my new friends and followers.

9

Egghead

I checked my phone the second I woke up. There were a few new comments, but I had posted pretty late, so I figured I'd get more today. I wanted to talk to Jasper about it on the bus, but he wasn't there for some reason. That was probably better anyway because I was really bored of talking about Lilly.

When we got to school, all the fifth-graders went directly to the cafeteria to set up our projects.

Now I knew why Jasper hadn't been on the bus. His project was huge. He had a stand-up trifold board, with the word "EROSION" at the top in the center, spelled out in block-letter stickers. Even from the doorway, I could see it looked great. When I got closer, I saw he had typed a whole page of explanation about his project and glued it on the left side, and in the middle under the word "EROSION," he'd used block-letter stickers to say:

WHICH MATERIAL WILL
ERODE MOST QUICKLY: WOOD,
CEMENT, OR PLASTIC?

Then he hypothesized that wood would erode most quickly, but in his conclusion, he explained that the cement had actually eroded the quickest. He had pasted pictures on the right side showing how he'd frozen and defrosted all three materials a few times. Seemed simple but looked amazing.

"Wow," I said to him. "Why didn't you tell me you had been working on this?" If he'd said something about it, I definitely wouldn't have forgotten.

"I dunno. You didn't ask." Fair point. "Plus, it only took a couple of minutes each day, so I didn't really think about it." I was really glad Mom wasn't there since she was always talking about working steadily: "Slow and steady wins the race," "Never put off until tomorrow what you can do today," blah, blah, blah.

Other kids were putting their projects on any tables with available space, so I walked up and down the aisles looking for a bad project to place mine next to so it would make mine look good.

I stopped short when I saw Zack setting up his project.

He had three glass jars. One was labeled "WATER" and was filled with water, except there was an egg inside it. Another was labeled "OLIVE OIL," and it had yellow oil along with an egg. The third was filled with dark liquid and didn't have an egg at the bottom, just some mush floating on top. It was labeled "SODA."

On his poster, I could see the pencil lines Zack had drawn to keep the words even. He'd written at the top, "WHICH IS WORSE FOR AN EGGSHELL: WATER, OLIVE OIL, or SODA?" In a different color on the next (straight) line, he wrote, "I hypothesize that soda will be the worst for an eggshell." And then, on the next line: "CONCLUSION: Soda is THE WORST."

I had to ask. "How'd you do this?"

"Well, back in September, after we got the assignment, I put an egg in each of these jars and put them on top of my bookshelf and forgot about them. When I took them down this week, the one in water was the same, the one in olive oil was a little yellowish, but mostly the same— but the soda one had completely dissolved. That gunk at the top is all that's left."

"Wait," I said. "Ms. Robinson only gave us the handout about the science fair three weeks ago. How could you have done this back in September?"

"Oh, my mom told me about it when she

got home from Back-to-School Night. And she told me she could prove that soda is as bad for me as she says. So we put the eggs in the jars then. I only started working on the poster when Ms. Robinson gave us the handout."

Well, I definitely wasn't going to put my project down next to *that*.

I found an empty table in the back corner, and I took the rubber band off my bright pink poster. The edges kept rolling back up, no matter how hard I tried to flatten them. It was probably as embarrassed as I was about how it looked.

I was rolling the poster back on itself when Matthew started setting up next to me.

He also just had a plain poster, but his was white and flat. At the top he'd written, "What food does a two-year-old like best?" Underneath that, it said, "I hypothesize that two-year-olds like cookies best." And underneath that: "Conclusion: Two-year-olds like cookies best." Then he'd taped pictures of his youngest sister, Zoe, picking up and eating cookies.

That was something else about Matthew: even though he was tough on his friends, he was always really nice to his younger sisters.

"That's it?" I asked. I was relieved his project was even dumber than mine. "You took pictures of Zoe eating cookies?"

"*No,*" Matthew said, rolling his eyes. "If you read the explanation of the project," he said, pointing to the piece of paper next to the poster, "you'd see that I put three different kinds of foods in bowls—broccoli, sweet potatoes, and cookies—and I watched to see which she grabbed first."

"Well, duh! Anyone would choose cookies."

"Oh, like no one would *ever* guess that a bouncy ball would bounce higher than a football." I guess he'd been watching me set up.

Mr. Brubaker's voice came over the loudspeaker. "OK, scientists. You should have now had enough time to set up your projects. You may now go to your lockers and then head straight to your homerooms so your teachers can take attendance and escort you to the auditorium for graduation practice."

That meant no class this morning! The cafeteria got all noisy with excited talk.

"Quiet!" Mr. Brubaker yelled into the microphone. "If you can't behave properly, you can't go to Dorney Park." Dead silence.

"That's better. Now, while you're in graduation practice, your teachers will come back here to grade your projects, then they'll pick you up after you're done and take you to class."

I took a deep breath. I really hoped Ms. Robinson would be an easy grader on this, although she always took a lot of points off for carelessness.

Then I remembered the elbow butt picture I'd posted last night. Everyone had thought it was funny, and I'd gotten a ton of new followers. I was betting that by the time I got to homeroom, people would be coming up to tell me how much they liked it. And not just my friends—some of the popular kids too.

But when I got to homeroom, everyone was crowded around Zack.

"Did the whole eggshell really dissolve?" Nelson asked.

"Yeah! There was nothing left at all except that gross stuff on the top!" You could hardly see Zack in the middle of the circle of kids because he was so much shorter than everyone else, but I could hear from his voice that he was psyched to have so much attention and to be grossing everyone else out in the process.

"Imagine what it does to your insides." He let it sink in. "That's why I never drink the stuff."

Pffft. The reason he never drank soda was because his mom didn't let him, not because of this dumb science project—which, come to think of it, sounded like it was his mom's idea too.

Danny was standing at the edge of the group. "Did you like the picture I took?" I asked him.

"Of the bouncy ball? It was a little blurry, but it was good, I guess," he said.

"No, not the pictures for the science fair. The picture of my elbow that you thought was my butt."

"Oh, yeah. That was funny." But he didn't sound like he thought it was funny, even though he had last night. He turned back to Zack.

"Well, I have an even funnier one," I said, making a mental note to find an even funnier one.

"OK," said Danny. "Whatever."

10

Bugging Out

Even though I was pretty hungry, I was not looking forward to dinner because I knew Mom and Dad would ask about the science fair.

Emmie asked if she could set the table. This was weird. Normally, Mom had to nag a couple of times before one of us did it, so I wasn't sure why she'd volunteered.

Mom must have been suspicious too, though, because she stopped stirring the pasta and turned around. "Why? Why do you want to set the table?"

"I have a treat I want to share with every-one," Emmie said.

"What kind of treat?"

"It's a surprise."

"Did you make it?" asked Mom.

Emmie got out the place mats while I mea-sured out food for Lucy and put it in her bowl. "No, Ms. Jerome gave us each some to take home."

Mom shrugged. "OK." I guess she figured that if it was from the teacher, it was fine. I, for one, was happy Emmie *wanted* to set the table instead of arguing with me about whose turn it was.

"Ms. Jerome said you can put it on a salad."

"Is it some kind of salad dressing?" I asked. I like creamy French. And that's it.

"No," she said. "You'll see."

Mom gave Emmie the salad bowl to put on the table. "Put it down gently," she warned. "The table is wobbly."

I saw Emmie sprinkle something on top of the salad, but I couldn't tell what.

"You can tell Daddy it's time for dinner," said Mom.

Emmie cupped her hands around her mouth. "Daddy! Dinner!" she yelled. Mom jumped.

"Not like that. I could have done that. Go to the family room and tell him nicely, please."

I knew I was about to be in for it. When we sat down at the table, I passed around the food so I didn't have to catch anyone's eye or have to talk.

"Who did something fun today?" asked Dad.

"I did something fun," said Emmie happily. "I went on a field trip to the Insectarium."

Mom looked up. "Oh! That was today?"

"Yeah? Tell us about it," said Dad.

"We went into the butterfly pavilion. It was like a thousand degrees in there, but it was *so* cool. We saw so many pretty butterflies. One landed on Analyn's head."

Analyn was the middle Rodef, between

Matthew and Zoe. She and Emmie were in kindergarten together, on-and-off friends, so I knew this time Emmie must be jealous.

"One butterfly landed right on Jordyn's mommy's tushy." She giggled. "I think it must have tickled because she was wearing yoga pants so she could probably feel it land."

Mom looked over at Dad. Dad didn't say a word.

Emmie was on a roll, and for once I was happy about it. "And we saw how a caterpillar turns into a butterfly. Can I collect caterpillars after dinner?"

"Uh, sure, I guess," said Dad.

"But leave them outside," Mom added.

"OK." Emmie took a big forkful of salad.

Then it happened. "Ezra! How was the science fair?" asked Dad.

"Wait," I said to Emmie, "when my class went, we saw tons of bees and beetles and spiders. Did you see those too?"

She nodded vigorously. "Oh, yeah." If I

played my cards right, I could maybe keep her talking all through dinner. Out of the corner of my eye, I noticed Dad still looking at me.

"What did you see?" I asked, as if this was the most fascinating topic ever.

"We saw how bees make honey! We saw them in the hive."

"No honeybees landed on Jordyn's mommy, I'm guessing," said Mom.

"Oh no, they were behind glass. So were the tarantulas. They were *so* gross. And we learned how people around the world eat insects for food." Emmie gave her a big smile. "The lady at the Insectarium gave Ms. Jerome some nacho-cheese mealworms that we could each take home. Don't they taste good?"

Mom, who had been eating salad, started gagging. She ran over to the sink and spat out what was in her mouth.

"*That's* what you put in the salad? Emerson Anne Miller! How could you?" Wow. *Emerson Anne Miller.* Not good, Emmie. I tried not to smile. Compared to tricking people into eating bugs, maybe a bad job on the science fair project wouldn't seem so terrible. "Did Ms. Jerome *tell* you to put bugs on our food?"

"No, she just said to give them to you," Emmie said, as if nothing was wrong. "But I tasted one, so I knew it tasted good. Everyone else in the class liked it too. Except Owen. He threw up."

Mom glared at her, and Emmie leaned really far back in her chair. "Do not ever put anything on anyone's food without telling them what it is. *Ever!*"

"OK, I won't." Emmie crossed her arms and stuck out her bottom lip. This was clearly not the response she'd expected.

Dad's mealwormy salad was still sitting on his plate. He pushed it away. "So, Ezra," he said, turning to me, "how'd the science fair go?"

I picked up my fork and took a bite of bug salad. It wasn't so bad, actually; it just tasted like crunchy nachos. "Yum!" I said.

Emmie grinned. Mom and Dad did not.

"Don't try to avoid the subject," Dad said. Mom was looking at me too.

I swallowed. "OK, I guess."

"You guess?" asked Mom. "You don't know? What grade did you get on it?"

"The teachers were working on the evaluations while we were at graduation practice, and we won't get grades back until Friday." That was one good thing, at least. Maybe Mom and Dad would have forgotten about this by then.

"Did you see any really good ones?" Dad asked.

"Zack's was very gross. He put raw eggs in soda, and they turned to mush. He said that's what happens to your insides if you drink soda."

Mom choked on the Diet Coke she was drinking to get the taste of bugs out of her mouth. "Zack said that, or his mom said that?"

I knew she wasn't a huge fan of Mrs. Zucker. Once, when Zack came over for a playdate, his mom said he never ate "processed poison" like the kind I always had for lunch. Mom made a joke about how she'd "keep poison off the menu today," but she never suggested I invite Zack over again.

"Yeah," I replied, "his mom probably told him to say that." Which was what Matthew and I had thought—and, anyway, I wanted Mom to know that she and I were on the same side. And she definitely didn't need to know how good Zack's project was.

"Any others?" asked Dad.

"Matthew's was dumb. He put broccoli, sweet potatoes, and cookies in front of his sister and then checked which she'd go for."

"Analyn was part of Matthew's experiment? Did you tell everyone that I helped with yours?" asked Emmie, uncrossing her arms.

"Not Analyn. Zoe."

"Well, did you tell everyone that I helped?"

"Yeah," I lied. No one would ever find out that I hadn't said anything about that, but I knew Mom and Dad would like it if I made Emmie happy.

"Well, that was nice," said Dad. "But you know, Ez, you really could have done a better job if you hadn't waited until the last minu—"

"I know! I was the one who had to go in with a pink poster." I fiddled with my napkin. "Anyway, I don't want to talk about it anymore."

"Well," Mom said, "if you don't want to have this conversation again, don't turn in work that we all know is not your best."

I pushed my plate away. We were all finished. Mom hadn't taken another bite since spitting out the salad.

"Can I go collect caterpillars?" Emmie asked.

"After you rinse your plate and put it in the dishwasher," Mom told her.

We cleared the table, and Emmie raced out the door. I headed back up to my room. A bunch of new comments had been added on my post since dinner.

ZACK: if you eat candy with castore-um in it, it came from a beaver's butt

JASPER: 👹

DANNY: 😫 😫 😫

A lot of the responses were from people I knew, but some were from strange usernames.

ZACK: IKR

I was the one who had taught Zack to abbreviate "I know, right?" and now he was using it as if he invented it. *So* annoying. Plus, it was obvious he was loving that people thought he was some kind of cool nerd scientist. He was probably making it up that they'd put something from a beaver's butt in food.

ME: ✕

ZACK: It is true

He put in a quote from an article saying castoreum, whatever that was, came from the glands of a beaver's butt. And then he made an Instagram story with a photo of a book cover about a beaver, and he circled the beaver's butt.

Butt pictures were *my* thing.

ME: ¯_(ツ)_/¯ still eatin 🍬🔍

I knew this would hurt Zack's feelings since everyone knew his mom wouldn't let him eat "poison" candy. I mean, the Zuckers gave out raisins on Halloween.

ZACK: u r what you eat

MATTHEW: 😂EzraBeaverbutt

Carter Williams thumbs-up reacted to it. When had Carter and Zack even gotten connected?

OK, fine. I would show them what a funny butt picture *really* looked like, and then they'd remember why they liked my posts so much—much more than Zack's stupid beaver butt.

I also needed to show them who *didn't* have a beaver butt.

After I closed my door, I pulled down my pants a little so the top of my butt crack was showing, held the phone behind my back, and snapped a photo. Considering I couldn't really see behind me, the picture looked good.

I already had my caption: "Not a beaver butt!" It would definitely remind everyone who had the best butt pictures, and I knew it would get a million likes, maybe even from all of the travel soccer kids. But right when I was about to post it, I kind of had a feeling that I probably shouldn't.

As I was thinking about it, Lucy scratched on the door. I let her in, and she flopped down on my floor and rolled onto her back with her tummy up in her "please scratch my belly" pose. She looked up at me with big eyes.

So I plugged my phone into the charger without hitting send.

Beaver Butt

All Friday morning I worried about my science fair grade, especially because Ms. Robinson didn't say anything about it. Finally, just before lunch, she picked up a stack of papers from her desk.

"OK, folks, these are the evaluations from the science fair!" My heart was beating a mile a minute. "I have to say," she continued, "it's obvious that many of you worked really hard to be creative and organized."

Her eyes swept the classroom as she was talking, and she seemed to stop for a second to look at Zack. I could have been imagining it, but it also seemed like she was trying not to look at me. That was just nerves though; it wasn't like my project was so terrible.

"As you know, this is worth fifty points. Three of you had perfect scores, so I want to take a second to congratulate Zack, Danny, and Sophie." She walked over to their desks to hand each of them their evaluations faceup for everyone in the class to see. "Our class had the most perfect scores of any of the fifth-grade homerooms, so you made me very proud!"

She continued, "For everyone else, I know a lot of you worked very hard but made some silly mistakes, like not double-checking your spelling. Even though you got some points off, I don't want you to think you did a bad job. Just be more careful in the future because the sixth-grade teachers expect a lot, and I want you to be prepared as you start middle school."

So I was just a little careless, that was all.

"There were only a few projects where you

didn't put in as much thought and time as we would have liked." I looked down. I mean, it couldn't have been that bad, but I didn't want to see the look on her face to be sure. "I hope that for those students this will be a learning process—not just to learn the scientific method, but also to provide a lesson in planning ahead and having good study skills, which you'll need for next year."

Yeah, study skills. Got it.

She started to pass the evaluations out but paused and said, "Remember, you'll need to have these evaluations signed by your parents."

Ugh. I had forgotten about that. Now I would have to show my parents the grade—which might not be terrible after all. "If you bring it back signed on Monday, you'll get an extra credit point."

Maybe that would be all I'd need to get a perfect score. There was still hope.

I lost that hope when she passed my evaluation back. She held it facedown, the opposite of the perfect ones she wanted everyone to see. I waited until she moved on to the next person before I slid the paper toward me.

I lifted the top corner to peek: 38/50. Next to it, she'd drawn a frowny face.

Thirty-eight out of fifty was the lowest grade I'd ever gotten, not including the times I'd forgotten and turned in a homework assignment late. Usually, school was pretty easy for me, even if I didn't work hard on something. Still, thirty-eight was a passing score.

But that frowny face . . . it made me frown. In fact, my eyes started to prickle because Ms. Robinson was so nice all the time and always used stickers that said things like "Great job!" and "Well done!" I guess she didn't have a "Not enough thought on this" sticker or one with a frown, so she had to draw it.

I blinked hard and tried to distract myself. Sophie's cheeks were red, and she looked like she was trying not to smile. She was usually quiet in class and probably wasn't used to

getting attention. Or, at least, not good attention—I'm sure she was happy when the mean
girls stopped picking on her.

Danny opened his eyes real wide and
slapped both of his cheeks like the *Home Alone*
kid because I think he was kind of embarrassed
and didn't exactly know how to react to being
singled out, so he went with being goofy about
it to make the other kids laugh. I purposely
didn't turn to look at Zack, but I could see him
out of the corner of my eye. He was beaming.

That might have been the worst part.

Suddenly—and for no reason that had anything to do with him actually being cool—the
other kids were noticing him, Carter was re-
sponding to his comments, and on top of it all,
he was getting singled out for good work by
Ms. Robinson.

At lunch he sat down at his normal spot, but
this time he wasn't putting out his lunch to see
who would trade.

"I heard you got a perfect score on your

science fair project," Nelson said to Zack. "Ms. Hirsh told us that there were three perfect scores in your class."

"Yeah." Zack was pretending like it was no big deal, but he could barely keep the smile off his face. "What'd you get?"

Nelson shrugged. "I got a forty-nine out of fifty because I spelled *hypothesis* wrong in three places. I didn't know it had a *y* in it. But Lilly and Jasper got perfect scores."

I looked around for Jasper and saw he was already in the lunch line, talking to Lilly. He was smiling. I wondered if they were talking about their perfect scores or whether he was going to have a graduation party.

"Who were the other perfect scores in your class?" Nelson asked.

"Me," said Danny. "And Sophie Bodinny."

"Sophie? I didn't know she was smart."

"Guess so," said Zack.

"Or maybe her parents did her project for her, unlike some of us," said Matthew, straight at

Zack. That wiped the smile off his face. "I didn't get any help. I had to do it all myself."

"Zoe helped you," Danny said, cracking up.

Matthew didn't seem to think it was funny. "I meant on the scientific part. Anyway, Zoe could have done a better job than Ezra did on his."

Wait a second, I thought. We were supposed to be on the same side! (And anyway, my project was my own idea; Dad had only helped a little.) Why was he putting me down for no reason? Maybe his project didn't even get a passing grade.

"What? I'm sure I did better than you did," I said, really hoping it was true.

"I got a thirty-nine. What'd you get, Beaver Butt?"

Some friend he was. "Same," I said, which would be true as soon as I got the evaluation signed.

Matthew shrugged. "Well, at least I don't have a beaver butt."

"Shut up, Matthew," I snapped. "Don't call

me Beaver Butt just 'cause you're mad you had a bad project."

"Yours was just as bad, and you're the one who said you'd eat cast iron."

"Castoreum," Zack corrected. I knew he couldn't help himself.

"Whatever," Matthew said. "You are what you eat. I bet you do have a hairy beaver butt."

Everyone at the whole table was completely quiet.

I really wished Jasper would stop talking to Lilly and come to the table. He would definitely be telling Matthew to stop being a jerk. Danny's eyes were big, and Zack looked from Matthew to me, not sure what was going to happen. I knew I didn't want to fight Matthew. I mean, I did want to punch him in his stupid mouth, but I didn't want him to punch me back.

"Ha ha," I said. "You're so funny." I thought maybe sarcasm would make him look dumb. "What do you want, a medal or a chest to pin it on?"

"He didn't deny it," Matthew told everyone, then turned to me. "Your butt must look like a beaver's."

Everyone was watching and waiting.

I rolled my eyes. "Duh. Obviously, I don't have a beaver butt. I can prove it."

"Yeah, right. What are you going to do, pull down your pants here in the cafeteria?"

"Noooo," I said. Even though we weren't supposed to take out our phones during school, drastic times called for drastic measures.

I unzipped the front of my backpack without looking down, so the cafeteria aides wouldn't see, and put my phone in my lap. Then I lowered my eyes and scrolled until I found the photo I had taken the night before.

I slipped the phone into my lunch bag and slid it over to Matthew. He took a look and started laughing. It was like he suddenly remembered we were actually friends.

"You're the one who said I needed different kinds of butts—so there you go."

"OK, I gotta hand it to you. That's a good one," he said, still smiling. I could tell he liked that I'd taken his advice. The other guys at the table started breathing again. "I'd say that is the most booty-ful picture I've seen. Get it? *Booty*-ful!"

I had to laugh too. Matthew could be really funny. Not as funny as me or Danny, but still funny.

"What is it?" asked Danny.

"Yeah," said Nelson. "Show me!"

Everyone wanted to laugh because it wasn't tense anymore.

Matthew passed my phone to Danny, whose laugh came out sounding more like a pig snort. Danny passed it to Nelson, who passed it to the rest of the table until it got back to Matthew.

"You have to send me that picture," he told me. "This is definitely your best one yet." He started to hand me the phone. "Wait, I can just send it to myself," he said, as he typed in his number and hit send.

"I want it too!" said Danny.

"Me too!" said Nelson.

Matthew pulled out his own phone, copied the photo he'd just received, and sent it to them. OK, *now* we were talking. The science fair was over, and everyone at the table wanted my pic. Back on top!

Zack knew it too. Even though he spent the last few minutes of lunch talking about how much better kale chips were for you than potato chips, nobody asked what was and what wasn't healthy, and no one asked to trade.

As the cafeteria aides made their way toward us, I grabbed my phone. The booty pic was still visible because the screen hadn't gone dark yet, but I managed to shove the phone into my backpack before they got to our table.

Jasper had finally stopped talking to Lilly and was sitting down, scarfing down his lunch before the bell rang. He took a giant bite of hamburger and then shoved in some fries before he looked up and noticed we were all smiling. "What'd I miss?" he mumbled.

"You shouldn't talk with your mouth full," said Zack. "You could choke." Yeah, I didn't know why I had been worried about his being popular. There was absolutely nothing cool about a nerd scientist. Or at least not *that* nerd scientist.

Mr. Popularity

When I got home, Emmie was on the front lawn looking for caterpillars. I stayed outside shooting hoops with kids on my street until Mom called us in for dinner.

That was when my good mood that had started at lunch ended. I had forgotten that I had to get my science fair evaluation signed.

Who would be least likely to yell about the grade? Dad, because he was the one who helped with it, after all, so he was partly responsible for the way it turned out. I prayed no one would mention it at dinner.

That prayer was not answered.

The second after we washed our hands and sat down at the table, the first thing out of Mom's mouth was: "So? Today's Friday. Did you get the grade back from the science fair?"

"Yeah," I said, and started eating.

"Well?" asked Dad. "How'd you do?"

I swallowed. "We did OK."

"We?" he said. "We who?" He sounded confused.

"You and me," I said. "And Emmie." I looked at Emmie for support. She smiled at me. That was good. I had one person on my side at least.

Dad laughed, but it wasn't a happy laugh. "Since Emmie and I weren't the ones who waited until the very last moment to get started, we can hardly take credit for the grade." He plopped more broccoli on his plate. "Which was what, by the way? I didn't hear you tell us what you got."

I couldn't avoid it anymore. "I got a thirty-eight out of fifty. But if you sign it, I'll get extra credit. I passed, so it's fine."

"Our definition of *fine* isn't 'didn't fail,'" said Mom. "If you'd worked hard and gotten a thirty-eight, then it would have been a different story, but Dad and I—and you—know that you're capable of doing a much better job when you put your mind to something."

I crossed my arms and didn't say another word. How many times were they going to give me this lecture? I really wished that we didn't have a no-phones-at-the-table rule. All I wanted to do was not have to look at them or talk to them, and playing on my phone would have been perfect for that.

Emmie talked on and on about the caterpillars she'd collected and how one was already a chrysalis and about the butterflies they'd become. I couldn't have cared less about the difference between monarch butterflies or red-spotted purples or whatever, but Emmie's typical monologue definitely helped tonight. Nobody noticed I wasn't talking.

After dinner Mom put out a bowl of cherries. The first one I saw was a double cherry—two cherries had grown together to form perfect butt cheeks. Until I started posting, it had never occurred to me just how many fruits could look like butts.

I put some cherries on my plate and, when no one was looking, put the stuck-together one in my pocket. As soon as I could, I went to my room and grabbed my phone.

I took the cherry butt picture and posted it with the caption, "My Cherry-Red Butt!"

I had forty-five new followers. Some of them were popular kids, and some I didn't know. I also had a bunch of likes from my old followers, and Lilly messaged me.

LILLY:

Is that really your butt?

Guess that pic of my elbow was still getting around.

ME:

No, it was my elbow

LILLY:

Not the elbow. The

other picture

ME:

The peach?

LILLY:

The one from today

ME:

???

The cherries? No way could she have seen that already. Then I wondered if Zack had posted another animal butt. I would be so mad if he did.

Her next text took a few seconds.

I saw the picture that I'd shown at lunch and was totally confused.

> **ME:**
>
> **Where'd you get that**

> **LILLY:**
>
> **From Peyton**

Peyton? I was kind of friends with him because we were on the same Little League team, but that was it. He didn't even go to Hughes anymore; he'd transferred to private school at the end of last year. How had he seen the pic? I hadn't posted it anywhere.

I couldn't tell if Lilly thought it was funny or not either, so I decided to play it safe.

> **ME:**
>
> **IDK**

> **LILLY:**
>
>

I didn't lie to her; I just hadn't exactly answered her question. And it was weird, her having seen my butt. I mean, I wouldn't have ever shown her the pic—gross!—but still.

There no time to think about it because my phone kept buzzing. I was getting lots of alerts about new followers. It was so cool. People were seeing my posts and telling their friends.

Everyone was finally noticing me.

"Ezra!" Mom called upstairs. "Bring me the science fair evaluation so I can sign it before we forget to do it over the weekend!" I didn't want to miss out on the extra credit or else I'd have one less point than Matthew. Even if Ms. Hirsh also gave credit for getting it signed and he was still one up on me, I definitely wanted that point.

I went downstairs and got the paper out of my backpack. Mom looked at the number and the frowny face, shook her head, and didn't say another word. She just signed it and handed it back.

POO-berty

I'd watched the numbers increase all weekend, and by the time I arrived at school on Monday, I had 175 new followers, bringing my total to over three hundred! I didn't even think the cherry butt picture was my best, but based on the numbers, it seemed the people had spoken.

So cool. It was a bummer that the school year was so close to being over since I wouldn't have time to hang out with all the kids who thought I was funny. Which I was.

When Ms. Robinson asked for our signed evaluations, I put mine facedown right on top of Zack's—who, of course, had put his faceup. His mom had signed her name real big and written, "Thank you!" on it and drawn her own smiley face. *Blech.*

A minute later Mr. Volpi came in. Ms. Robinson didn't leave this time. Instead, she said, "OK, folks, settle down. We're dividing up for health class today. Boys, you're going to stay here with Mr. Volpi. Girls, I'm going to walk you to the gym where Ms. Pollock will be teaching you." Ms. Pollock was one of the other gym teachers.

"I bet this is when the girls hear about their periods," Danny whispered. Danny is not good at whispering, so everyone heard him.

As soon as the girls left, Mr. Volpi picked up a marker and wrote "PUBERTY" on the board.

He turned back toward us. "Who knows what puberty is?"

At my last checkup, Dr. Gordon had talked to Mom about how I might start to get acne soon when I "entered puberty," but Dr. Gordon pronounced it, "PEW-berty." Mr. Volpi said it like, "POO-berty." A couple of the guys started giggling, but I couldn't tell if they were laughing because they knew what puberty was or because Mr. Volpi had said "poo." Either way, I was just praying I wouldn't get called on.

"Anyone?" Nobody raised a hand. "Fine," he said. "Puberty is when your body starts to change. You'll get taller, and you'll get acne, and you'll start to grow hair. Any of you notice you're growing hair where you weren't before? Like on your face or under your arms? Or on your privates?"

He looked at us, waiting. Seriously, was he out of his mind? Did he actually think anyone would tell him if they had hair on their privates? I wouldn't even look up because then I might have accidentally caught his eye and gotten called on.

"No volunteers, eh? Well, it's probably already starting to happen to you."

I sneaked a look around. Zack was sitting

with his eyes wide and his mouth hanging open like he didn't really understand the whole concept. Mr. Volpi noticed, of course. "Well, most of you, at least. But don't worry, it happens to everyone sooner or later." He nodded at Zack. If Zack was as mortified as he should have been, it wasn't obvious. "So there's a slideshow I have to show you now. Can someone get the lights?"

The first slide was a drawing of the side view of a man's privates with everything labeled. Mr. Volpi pointed out the parts of the diagram, using scientific terms like *vas deferens*. It was hard to believe that a subject that was so embarrassing could also be so boring at the same time.

I really wished I could check my phone. All I wanted to do was see how many new friends I had and also to have someplace to look other than the slideshow or the other guys. I'd had the phone for only a few weeks, and now I couldn't really remember what life had been like without it.

Then I realized something: even though all these new people were interested in my posts, Jasper—my best friend—hadn't texted or talked to me about any of it. He only wanted to talk about Lilly. Well, if he was going to start paying more attention to her, I had lots of other people to hang out with.

Mr. Volpi got a coughing fit that stopped him from talking, and he left the room to get some water. No one said a word. We didn't even look at each other. I didn't know how anyone else was reacting, and I didn't really know whether I was supposed to be interested in this or not (but I really was not). Maybe the other guys were thinking the same thing.

We just sat there until Mr. Volpi got back. He finished the slides on the private parts and the ways and times they would grow and change, which was beyond embarrassing, and then moved on to how our Adam's apples would get bigger.

Danny spoke up as usual. "I can see mine

when I turn sideways. But mine's a Danny's apple, not an Adam's apple," he said, laughing. Some of the other guys laughed too. I just wanted this to be over.

Mr. Volpi didn't yell at him. All he said was, "All right, son, very funny."

Then he told us how our voices would get deeper and where hair would grow. More hair. So much hair. I hoped I never grew any, at least not in the embarrassing places. Facial hair would be cool though. That way, I wouldn't have to keep drawing the mustache on. Maybe next time I'd do a soul patch under my bottom lip.

After the last slide, Mr. Volpi talked about acne and hygiene (again), as if we hadn't heard enough. He turned off the slides but didn't tell anyone to get the lights.

Instead, he sat on Ms. Robinson's desk and said in a quiet voice, like he was sharing a secret, "Listen up, boys." I was in the last row, so I had to lean in a little to hear him. "The girls are getting a talk about getting their periods.

You don't need to know the details about that. You don't *want* to know the details about that."

I heard the door opening behind me. Ms. Robinson walked in quietly and sat down nearby. Mr. Volpi didn't see her. He kept talking.

"All I will say is that when you start dating and get married, if your girl starts to get a little crazy, you just need to know that she's probably on her period, so the best thing to do is just be nice and don't argue, and she'll calm down eventually."

I sneaked a look at Ms. Robinson. Her eyes were as round as I'd ever seen, her mouth was open with surprise, and she gasped a little, which finally got Mr. Volpi's attention. He nodded at her and didn't seem to notice that she looked mad—but I noticed.

"OK, guys, that's all. Remember, wear deodorant. You do need it, even if you think you don't." He told someone to turn on the lights. "Ms. Robinson, we're done here. You can bring the girls back in when they're ready."

She gave him a look—I could see she was still mad—and marched out. Five minutes later, she came back with the girls, who each carried a little brown bag with handles.

"They got gifts?" Danny whispered, loudly enough for everyone to hear. None of the girls looked at him. They just kept their eyes down and took their seats.

The bell rang.

I'd never been so happy to see Senorita Goldberg come through the door.

Maxi Face

At lunchtime Zack sat down in Matthew's place. I didn't know what he was thinking; he should have realized that any special treatment he had gotten for his science fair project was long over.

"Move!" Matthew said when he showed up, and Zack immediately moved without arguing.

Matthew had something under his shirt. "Look," he said, as he pulled out a small brown bag with handles—the same kind the girls had brought back with them at the end of health class.

"Is that what the girls had?" asked Zack. "How'd you get that?"

"Someone threw it in the trash, so I picked it out when no one was looking," Matthew said, smiling proudly.

Zack wrinkled his nose. "You should probably wash your hands before you eat lunch."

"Pfft." Matthew blew him off, then opened the bag and looked in.

"What is it?" asked Jasper.

"Looks like some coupons for"—Matthew read the coupons—"Kimberly-Clark products? Who's Kimberly Clark?" Next, he pulled out a small plain cardboard box. The words "maxi pad" were printed on it. I didn't know what that was. No one else seemed to know either.

"Open it," Danny said. Just then, one of the lunch aides started to walk down the row. Matthew quickly hid the box on his lap. Once she got busy two tables away telling some kids to clean up the milk they had spilled, he took it out again.

Inside was something puffy and folded over. He unfolded it, and we all stared. The thing was soft like a paper napkin on one side, and on the other side was a shiny piece of paper with the words "Remove to Expose Adhesive." Matthew removed it, and sure enough, that side was sticky—but not too much. It was like a sticky note. When he touched it, it stuck to his finger but came right off.

I grabbed it out of Matthew's hands, stuck it on my chin, and curved it around the bottom of my face. It almost reached from ear to ear.

"Ho ho ho," I said. "I'm Santa Claus!" Everyone started laughing. Zack laughed so hard he got the hiccups. I really wished someone would take a pic.

The lunch aide looked over to see what all the ruckus was about. I tore off the maxi pad, but I was pretty sure she'd seen.

She kept looking at me. It felt like she was looking forever.

She didn't come over but went to another lunch aide and started talking to him, nodding in our direction. My heart was pounding.

The bell rang, and I practically ran back to class. All afternoon I waited to see if I was going to get in trouble, but I didn't get called down to the office, and I finally breathed a sigh of relief when I got on the bus.

A strange car was in the driveway when I got home, and my heart started pounding again.

Then Nana and Pop came out of the house.

I'd totally forgotten they were arriving a week early for a visit before my graduation since they were driving all the way from Florida and then staying until it was time for Emmie's.

"Wow," said Pop when he saw me. "You got huge, champ."

Nana moved in for a kiss. I was glad the bus had left by then. "Oh my goodness!" she said. "I practically have to stand on my tiptoes to kiss your forehead."

"Let's stand back-to-back." I wanted to see if I was taller than she was. Nana turned around. I lifted my chin to get every millimeter and put my hand across the tops of both of our heads. Just about even.

"You're going to be twice Nana's size this time next year," Pop said. "Of course, she's a little munchkin." He laughed.

Nana didn't laugh. "Well, I don't know about *munchkin*."

Pop was quiet for a second. He must have gone a little too far. Then he waved his arm toward the house and said, "C'mon in. We have graduation presents for you."

Dad had come home early, so he was already sitting at the kitchen table with Emmie, who was painting her fingernails with nail polish.

"Look at what Nana and Pop got me." She held up her hand. "It's pink!" she said, with a huge smile. I pretended to care so Dad wouldn't tell me to use my manners in front of Nana and Pop.

"I thought you were going to save the polish for your graduation," said Pop.

"That's not till next Thursday," Emmie whined. "And anyways, if I want to wear it to my graduation, I need to practice putting it on now." Sounded like pretty dumb logic to me, but whatever.

Nana smiled at her and said, "Of course, it's fine for you to wear it now. If you run out before Thursday, we'll get you more." That made Emmie smile again. Great, she was getting all the nail polish she wanted. Nobody had said anything about my graduation.

I looked at Nana.

"We have a graduation present for you too, of course, Ez," said Nana, excitedly. Pop handed me a flat box. I really hoped it wasn't what I thought it was, 'cause it sure looked like a dress shirt, like one I'd have to wear to graduation.

I pretended to be excited about it, but then, wow! It was way better than a dress shirt—it was a Roy Halladay commemorative Phillies jersey.

"Thank you so much!" I said, and I really meant it.

I put on the new jersey. Even with the T-shirt

I wore to school underneath it, it was big, but I loved it.

"Hello, hello," Mom said, walking into the kitchen. "Welcome!" She hugged Nana, then turned to Pop and said, "Hey, Dad," and gave him a kiss. "I'm glad you guys are here. Let me go upstairs and get changed. And then who wants to go to Elly Fants?"

"I do!" Emmie and I both said at the same time.

Unwelcome Attention

By the time I woke up the next morning, I had five hundred followers—almost as many people as in my whole entire school! Most of the younger kids didn't have phones, so word about me must have gotten out.

I bet even Carter didn't have as many followers as I did now. I was on my way to becoming a viral sensation.

Most of the names were unfamiliar, but I figured once the popular kids had started following me, their friends from other schools on the travel soccer team did too. Some of them were pretty dumb, like one who said, "show ur butt," someone else who said, "ur a butt," and even a really mean one who said, "butthead." I just blocked them. They were nothing compared to the *almost five hundred* who were loving my posts.

Man, I wished I'd had the phone before the treasurer election last year—I definitely would have won.

When Jasper and I walked into school, I could tell that people knew about my posts because I saw some kids whispering to each other. It was a little weird they didn't say hi, but I guess when you're getting well-known, people treat you better and are even a little afraid to make eye contact. This had to be what the popular kids felt like. I saw Carter down the hall, and he didn't wave, but he probably hadn't seen me.

Right after homeroom we had to go to the auditorium for another graduation practice. I mean, don't get me wrong—I was happy not to have to learn anything, but it was kind of boring just sitting around until your name was called and then going up on stage.

Mr. Brubaker wasn't in the auditorium. Instead, Ms. Pollock was standing on the stage trying to get everyone to settle down.

"*Shhh!* Folks, please be quiet," she said loudly into the microphone. Barely anyone stopped talking.

Never make a gym teacher tell you anything twice. She waited about two seconds, then blew her whistle into the microphone. Zack clapped his hands over his ears and almost dropped to the floor.

"Thank you," she said, as if the reason we were quiet was because we were minding our manners and not because she'd just burst our eardrums. "Places, everybody." She raised her arms so that the kids with the "A" names would stand up.

This time, Ms. Callaghan, the music teacher, was at the piano at the front of the stage.

"Ms. Callaghan, 'Pomp and Circumstance,' please," Ms. Pollock said as she nodded toward the piano. I recognized the song Ms. Callaghan started playing—da da da-da-da *daaaaaah* da—from all the TV shows that had graduation ceremonies. It was kind of cool, actually.

When it was time for the M's to line up, Lilly wasn't there. "Where's Lilly?" I asked Jasper, who shared her homeroom.

"She got called down to Brubaker's office, and I guess she's not back yet."

That would explain why Mr. Brubaker wasn't there either.

Lilly was never in trouble, so I figured maybe she was getting a special award or a part at graduation, which wouldn't have surprised me because she was one of the best students in our grade. I really hoped she'd be back by the end of practice, or at least that I wouldn't have to get a different partner. If I had to have Molly Murtaugh, that would be really bad.

Molly was standing next to Jasper, and

before I turned back around, she said, "Hey, butthead." I didn't know if that was her way of being funny or trying to pretend to be cool because I was getting popular, but it was not funny. "Are you going to show us your butt or just send us a picture?" She kind of sneered when she said it.

"What?" I said. She really was awful. I couldn't understand why anyone put up with her, much less the popular girls.

"Everyone knows it's your butt."

"You mean the cherries? You thought that was my butt because I wrote 'my cherry-red butt'?"

"I know it was cherries. They were *red*. Not like your actual butt, which you're showing everyone."

Now I was getting a little worried, remembering Lilly's text last night. She had gotten the picture from Peyton, who'd gotten it from . . . somewhere? Jasper didn't say anything. He just looked down at his feet. But who cared what Molly thought, anyway?

Luckily, we were starting to walk down the aisle, and when we got to the front, I turned one way and she turned the other. I took my place and looked to see who was coming, but most people just kept their eyes forward.

Alex came down the aisle, and when he got to my row, he slapped his own butt and stuck it out at me. The kids behind him all laughed.

My stomach did a flip. I saw a boy whisper something in his ear when they went into their row. They both looked back at me and laughed. I tried to make my eyes go blurry so I wouldn't get tears in them.

I spent the rest of graduation practice making sure no one else would look at me funny or say anything mean. I wished I had my phone.

I didn't get it. What had happened?

My homeroom was dismissed after practice to go right to gym class, which normally would have been great, but my heart, which had calmed down a little bit, started pounding again at the thought of being around all the kids where they could say mean stuff to me. I didn't want to talk to anyone except my friends.

As we passed the main office, I saw Mr. Brubaker talking with Lilly and Mr. and Mrs. Mensh. I was so relieved.

"Hey, Lilly," I said after he went back into the office. She saw me, quickly looked away, and left the building with her parents.

Just when I could have used a friend to remind me that the mean girls and the popular boys were dumb—which I already knew but somehow had forgotten when they had started being nice to me—she didn't even say hello. I hoped everything was OK with her family. Maybe she had to go home because of an emergency and that's why she was at the office? Now I was even more nervous.

Thankfully, nothing happened during gym. We had to take the PACER test, so we all ran the whole time, and no one could talk. By the time it was done, everyone was sweaty and tired.

We went back to our homerooms to get our lunch bags. I wasn't at all hungry. In fact, my stomach kind of hurt. Still, it would be a relief to see my friends.

When I walked into the cafeteria, I could see that Zack was back to trying to trade away his lunch. As I passed one of the girls' tables, one of them whispered loudly, "He's going to put his butt on you!" and the other girls giggled. I pretended not to hear.

Everyone looked up when I got to the table, except Danny. Matthew wasn't there, which was weird because I had seen him from across the auditorium at graduation practice.

"Hey," I said, trying to be casual.

"Hey," Danny said, his eyes on his tray.

"Do you have potato chips? I'll trade for these," said Zack, still trying to pawn off the gross kale chips.

I tossed him my chips. "You can keep yours," I said. "I'm not hun—"

My head was pushed forward by someone's

elbow. I saw Alex pass by, pretending it was an accident.

"Oh, sorry, *butthead*," he said, and laughed. He sat down next to Carter at their table, and Carter was laughing too.

"Ignore him," Jasper told me. "He's a jerk."

I nodded but kept my head down for the rest of lunch. I couldn't really eat. People were whispering and laughing about me. I bit my lip until it hurt, which kept me from tearing up.

When the bell rang, I threw out everything except the Oreos, which I gave to Zack because I knew he'd want them and because it was nice of him not to be weird with me. I mean, for once Zack's normal weirdness was actually good.

The rest of the afternoon crawled by—language arts, science, and social studies. All boring, but just sitting at my desk and listening to Ms. Robinson was fine. None of the kids could bother me.

In social studies she handed out worksheets

on our Constitutional rights and said we could do them in class; whatever we didn't finish would be our homework. We were all concentrating so we could get them done as fast as possible.

When the classroom phone rang, it startled me. Everyone looked up.

Ms. Robinson spoke quietly into the phone for a minute. I went back to work because there was less than a half hour left, and I really didn't want to take this home.

But then she hung up and said, "Ezra, please take your things and go down to Mr. Brubaker's office. You'll be dismissed to go home from there."

OK, that was weird. But I was happy about it because at least if I walked out to the bus with Mr. Brubaker after school, no one would be able to say mean things or push me.

The Detective

I couldn't figure out why Mr. Brubaker wanted to see me. Did one of the aides tell him about the kids being mean at lunch? I wasn't going to tattle on them—that was for sure. But then my stomach dropped. Maybe the aide had reported me for yesterday's maxi pad incident after all.

Ms. Segal, the school secretary, was at her desk in front of Mr. Brubaker's closed door.

"Hi, Ezra. You can wait for Mr. Brubaker on the bench next to your parents."

My parents? She nodded toward the bench

behind me. I turned around, but before anyone could say anything, the door opened and Matthew and his mom walked out. Like Lilly, he pretended not even to see me.

What was this? The people I wanted to talk to were ignoring me, and the people I didn't want to talk to wouldn't leave me alone.

My mind was going a mile a minute trying to figure out what Mom and Dad were doing here and what Mr. Brubaker had called us in for. I couldn't even look at them. I didn't want them to know other kids were being mean to me, and I *really* didn't want them to know I had put a maxi pad on my face in school.

Mr. Brubaker was in front of his desk. He shook hands with Mom and Dad, and then he looked at me.

There were four chairs set up in front of the desk, and a woman who looked kind of familiar was in the chair all the way to the right. She was wearing a button-down shirt and a pair of black pants like Mom wore for work. My parents noticed her at the same time.

While Mr. Brubaker shut the door, she stood up. "Connie Kelly," she said as she shook my parents' hands.

"Let's sit down." Mr. Brubaker motioned to the other three chairs. "Thank you for coming in, Mr. and Mrs. Miller. Ezra."

We all sat down.

"You may already know Detective Kelly," Mr. Brubaker said to Mom and Dad. *Detective* Kelly. Mom's eyes got a little wide.

"My daughter, Maeve, is in second grade here," she told us. Why would I know her daughter? I wasn't sure why that mattered, or why we were meeting with her at all. "But I'm here in my official capacity, unfortunately," she continued. They called the police because I put a maxi pad on my face? Really?

"Detective?" said Dad, who looked as confused as I felt.

Detective Kelly kept going. "Mr. and Mrs.

Miller, I'm sure this will come as a shock, but we have information that at least one lewd photo was taken and sent from your son's phone."

"Wait, what?" I said. No one took any photos of the maxi pad on my face. This didn't make any sense. "What's 'lood'?"

"'Lewd' means it's a dirty picture. A naked photo, in this case, honey," said Detective Kelly. I was glad she called me "honey" because I could tell she was trying to be nice, but *what?!*

Mom gasped. Dad shook his head like he didn't understand. "That can't be," he said. He looked at Mom, then turned to look at me.

"Did you send naked photos to anyone?" he said at the same exact second Mom asked, "A naked picture of whom?"

"Well, that's the question," said Detective Kelly. "We believe the photo was of your son's naked buttocks."

It was horrible, but I also had to stop myself from laughing. She'd said, "buttocks." But then they all looked at me, and I didn't have to stop myself from laughing anymore. Now I wanted to throw up.

"Ezra! What did you do?" Dad's voice was sharp.

"Nothing!" I said as I realized this wasn't about the maxi pad. "I didn't. I posted things that looked like butts on Instagram. I thought it was funny. I did the picture of Emmie's chicken nuggets from Elly Fants. And a peach, and the lines in my hand, and the inside of my elbow. And then I did post a picture of two cherries stuck together that I said was 'my cherry-red butt,' but it wasn't my butt! It was cherries."

"Oh," said Mom with a sigh of relief.

"This sounds like a misunderstanding, Detective. You know how it is when rumors spread," said Dad, who was almost smiling.

Detective Kelly shook her head. "I wish it were, Mr. Miller." She reached for a file on Mr. Brubaker's desk. Inside was a full-page color copy of the picture of the top of my butt crack, the one I showed at lunch to prove I didn't have a beaver butt.

Then their eyes were on me.

Dad's almost-smile was gone. "What is this?"

Mom put a hand on his arm. "Calm down, Paul. I'm sure that Ezra can explain."

"I . . . I took it because the kids were teasing me. But I didn't send it to anyone! I swear." I was shaking inside. No one said anything. They just kept staring at me. "Matthew called me a beaver butt, and I just took it to show them that I didn't have a beaver butt. But I *showed* it—I didn't send it."

"Well, how did they get it?" asked Dad.

"Matthew thought it was so funny he took my phone and sent it to himself, and some of the other kids wanted it, so I guess he forwarded it to them too. But I didn't send it! It wasn't me."

I was so mad. It wasn't my fault it had gotten sent.

Dad's voice got loud. "What do you mean

it wasn't you? It's a picture of *you*. *You* took a picture of your behind, Ezra. *You* were showing it to people."

I couldn't hold it in anymore. I started crying. I rubbed my eyes, but the tears kept coming.

It was all so terrible. It all suddenly made sense. The picture of my actual butt was forwarded and forwarded. That's how Peyton and Lilly saw it—and maybe everyone else. Including the popular kids. And they weren't laughing at my posts, they were laughing at *me*. I thought they liked me and that they'd start inviting me to do stuff with them. The stuff they were doing together was probably talking about how to make fun of me.

Detective Kelly spoke up. "Well, even if you didn't hit send, what most people—kids and adults—don't realize is that it's not just about sending out the photo. It's also a crime to take a lewd photo of a minor—someone under the age of eighteen," she added for me. "So that means that whoever takes a naked picture of a minor has committed a crime—even if the person is taking a picture of him- or herself."

I put my hands up to cover my eyes. I was crying so hard I couldn't breathe. Mom put her arm around my shoulder and pulled me toward her. "*Shhhh*," she whispered. "We'll get through this."

"How many people have seen the photo?" Dad asked the detective.

"We're not sure yet. Although he seems to have a lot of Instagram followers—"

I couldn't believe a police officer had seen my Instagram and all my posts. Everyone was looking at my posts, including adults. Including all those people I didn't even know. Including the people I *did* know, like Carter and Alex and Molly Murtaugh and Mom and Dad and Detective Kelly and Mr. Brubaker . . .

"—that picture wasn't on it. So it's not as many as it could be," Detective Kelly answered. "So far, it seems like only fifteen kids received it, and they all received it by text. It wasn't posted on any other social media, as far as we can tell. Of the fifteen kids who did receive it, one just sent it back to your son, and then they deleted it."

Oh no! That was Lilly. *That's* why she'd had to see Mr. Brubaker this morning. My picture was the reason she got in trouble.

"And one of the kids who received it showed it to a trusted adult, who brought it to our attention."

A kid showed it to an adult? Who? Was it Zack? But Zack had laughed about it and didn't seem to think it was a big deal. Or wait, maybe it was Peyton. But that didn't make sense because I knew he'd sent it to Lilly. What if it was a girl? Like Sophie. And what if she'd shown it to the popular kids?

I didn't want to ask who it was because I was really afraid of the answer.

"We made sure it was deleted off that kid's phone, and they aren't in trouble. But in order for us to know the extent of this, and to stop it from spreading any further, we've asked all the parents involved to let us take their children's phones and search them. And I'm asking you too," she finished.

Mom and Dad looked at each other. "I don't know, Detective," said Dad.

"Well, you don't have to give it to me. If you refuse, I'll have to ask a judge to give me a warrant to get it." She gave my parents a serious look. "I'm not here to give you legal advice. But I'm asking for access to your son's phone because I believe we'll find the picture I showed you—and I think that, like us, you'd also like to know what else, if anything, is there."

"Nothing! There's nothing else on it, I swear," I said, my voice cracking.

Dad ignored me. "What are the possible legal consequences, Detective?"

"Listen, Mr. Miller, I'm not going to lie to you. This is a serious situation. And I can't make any promises, because it's going to depend on what we find when we get into the phone. If we find more nude pictures on it, or anything that involved any sex act"—I could feel my face get hot—"or if we find any photos that were taken and sent around to harass, then we'd need to consider harsher punishments. But—"

"What's 'harass'?" I was almost afraid to ask.

"It means to bully someone or scare them on purpose," she said.

"I didn't. There isn't." I mean, *I* was the one who was harassed—first by Matthew, which got me to take and show the picture in the first place, and then by the kids who were making fun of me.

Detective Kelly looked me in the eye and nodded. "OK." She turned back to my parents. "Look, we don't want to give these kids criminal records. Assuming that there's nothing on your son's phone other than the photo we know about, we intend to delete it from his and everyone else's phones, and then make the kids who forwarded it take a mandatory state education program on internet safety. Once they've completed the program, we'd send a notice that the matter is officially closed and seal the record." She paused. No one said a word. "I can't make any promises until we've completed the investigation, but this really sounds like it was never intended to do any harm."

Mr. Brubaker chimed in, "I do also have to tell you, though, that the school has rules about cell phone usage—both during school and outside of school. So once the legal investigation is completed, I'll let you know what the school punishment will be. For now, we're going to send Ezra home, and he's suspended until the investigation is completed."

"Will you turn over the phone and provide the password?" Detective Kelly asked my parents.

Mom spoke up. "Can we have a minute to discuss this among ourselves?"

"Sure," said Detective Kelly.

"You can stay in here and talk," Mr. Brubaker told us. "Just come out to Ms. Segal's desk when you've decided."

After they closed the door behind them, I put my head down on the desk. I could hear Mom fishing around in her purse. She tapped me on the shoulder and handed me a tissue.

I turned away and blew my nose. It was totally quiet, except for me sniffling. I almost thought they weren't going to say anything, so I looked to see what they were doing. They were looking right back at me.

My father didn't seem as angry now. "Look, Ezra, I had to fire a guy last month because he sent dirty jokes to his friends in the office from his work computer. Even adults make mistakes about stuff like this. But I thought you'd know you should never, ever take or keep or send pictures like these. There are too many ways they can come back to haunt you."

He was lecturing me, but at least he wasn't yelling.

I bit my lip hard. "I know. I'll never, ever do it again. I swear."

"OK." He took a deep breath. "Right now we need to figure out what to do here. What do you think, Lisa?"

Mom's face was serious. "Ezra, we're here to protect you," she said. "You need to be completely honest and tell us if there's anything else on the phone."

"No. I swear!" I took the phone out of my backpack and opened the photo app. "Here, look at it." She scrolled through with Dad watching over her shoulder.

When they were done, she said to him, "I think we should turn it over." Dad nodded. He got up and opened the door, then motioned to Detective Kelly and Mr. Brubaker, who were chatting with each other.

Ms. Segal had a line of kids and adults waiting to talk to her about normal everyday things as if this was a normal day. I turned around quickly so no one would see me in the office.

Dad handed my phone to Detective Kelly.

"What's your password, honey?" she asked.

"One-one-one-one," I told her.

Detective Kelly looked at my parents, who seemed kind of embarrassed.

Dad cleared his throat. "Yeah, I can see now we haven't done a great job of teaching him what he needs to know about protecting himself when he's using a cell phone."

"Mr. Miller," Detective Kelly replied, "you'd be amazed how few parents do." She put the file folder and my phone in her briefcase, which was on the floor by her chair. "We'll be in touch with you in a few days after we've gone through this and completed the investigation."

I wasn't crying anymore, but I was so mad. That picture had just been a joke! All I did was show it to my friends. I hadn't sent it to anyone. Now all these other people had seen it, a lot of kids were in trouble, and I was suspended—maybe worse.

And now I had to walk out of the office, and I didn't know who I'd see.

A Hero to Someone

I tried not to look anyone in the eye as we walked out of the office, down the corridor, and out the door. I guess Mom and Dad had each been at work when the school called; they'd driven separately. Since Mom's car was closer to the entrance, I went home with her.

Neither of us said one word the whole drive. When we pulled up to our house, I saw Emmie out in the front yard collecting cater-pillars. And then I saw Nana and Pop's car in the driveway.

I got tears in my eyes again when I thought

about having to tell them what happened. My stomach hurt.

Mom's voice was gentle. "You know what, Ezra, why don't you help Emmie collect caterpillars while I say hello to Nana and Pop." I took a deep breath. Who'd have thought I'd ever want to help Emmie collect caterpillars? But right then I felt so relieved.

"Ezra," Emmie said the minute I got close enough, "look at this hairy caterpillar I found! I wonder what color butterfly it will be?" She was so focused on the caterpillar she didn't even look at my face or see that my eyes were still a little wet from crying. "I'm going to put it with the rest of them," she said, reaching for something. But whatever she wanted wasn't there.

"Where'd it go?"

"Where did what go?"

"My Junior Bug Collector container," she said. I must have looked confused because she added, "You know. The one I got for your birthday?"

"Wait, you mean the kit that Zack gave me?" I couldn't believe it.

"You gave it to me," she said, as if I was going to try to take it back. *Ha.* As if.

"Oh, yeah, it's totally fine. All yours. I just didn't think you'd really use it."

"Well, I am. But I put it right here." She looked down at the same spot as if it would just magically appear. Then, at the exact same minute, we both heard the bush rustle.

I realized what had happened to the bug container.

"Luuuuucy," I said in the voice we used when we wanted her to come. "C'mon out, girl."

Lucy appeared from behind the bush. In her mouth was the bug collection container. Her teeth had sunk into the top where the mesh was, and part of the lid was bent up, but it looked like it was still closed. I could see the caterpillars were still inside.

"Get it!" Emmie yelled.

Lucy sat down with her tail wagging, excited by all the attention. My sister ran toward her. For an old dog, Lucy still had some moves, and she cut to the side. She didn't see I was on her other side though, so as she turned from Emmie, she ran right into me. I grabbed her collar.

"It's OK, girl. Just drop it. Drop it." With my other hand, I pried the collection container out of her mouth. She sat down and then rolled onto her back. I handed the container to my sister and bent down so I could scratch Lucy's belly.

Emmie examined the container. There were holes at the top from Lucy's teeth, but the caterpillars were all fine, as was the chrysalis hanging from the top of the mesh. She opened it and dropped in the hairy caterpillar she was still holding. The top didn't screw on completely because Lucy's bite had warped it a little, but everything else was OK.

"Thank you, Ezra!" she said. "You saved the caterpillars. They can grow up and become butterflies!" She rushed over to where I was still sitting on the ground scratching Lucy and hugged me around my shoulders.

Emmie was the first person who had been happy with me since this whole terrible day had started. Not gonna lie, I didn't even try to get out of her hug.

I wondered what people knew about what happened at school. I wondered if anyone was trying to call me. I wondered if Detective Kelly would answer if it rang or if it would just go to voice mail. I wondered who else was trying to text me. I wondered if people were texting mean things. I hoped Detective Kelly saw those texts. It would serve them right if the police saw what they were saying to me. Tears came to my eyes again.

"Are you crying, Ezra? What's wrong? Are you sad?" asked Emmie.

I swiped at my face. "I'm not crying. I just had some of Lucy's hair in my eyes."

"Oh, good. I'm glad you're not sad," she

said, which also made exactly one person who cared about my not being sad.

● ● ●

As soon as we went into the kitchen, I could tell that my parents had told Nana and Pop what had happened because Nana hugged me. Pop said, "Hard day, eh, champ?" I nodded.

Luckily, we didn't talk about it at dinner, which I couldn't eat because my stomach was so queasy. Afterward, Dad and Pop went into the family room and turned on the Phillies game. I watched with them until it was my bedtime.

I usually argued to stay up until the game was over. Not this time. I just went to my bed-room when I was told, put on my pajamas, and didn't plug in my phone because I didn't have it. When Mom came in, I saw her look over at the table to make sure it was plugged in, the way she did every night, and I could see her remember that the police had it.

She kissed my forehead and said, "Good night, Ezra. We love you. I know your dad already told you that even adults make mistakes—but I want to be clear about it. *People* make mistakes. No matter what happens, we will get through this—*you* will get through this—and we love you." She kissed my forehead and turned out the light.

I lay there for a long time. I couldn't stop thinking.

I didn't know if I'd ever see the inside of Hughes Elementary again since I might be suspended for the rest of the year. Which was fine with me since I couldn't think of anyone I'd want to see. I definitely didn't want to see any of those mean popular kids again.

And I didn't want to see Matthew because he was the one who had started the whole thing. If he hadn't called me a beaver butt or teased me about my science project when his was just as bad, I wouldn't have taken the picture, which meant I wouldn't have shown it to him.

He was the one who sent it around. This was all his fault.

Then I started worrying that my picture had gotten Lilly in trouble too, and maybe she was mad at me. I didn't know about any of my other friends.

I tried to get my mind to think about anything else. The only thing I could come up with was Emmie's butterflies. I was still trying to picture them when I drifted off to sleep.

Oh, Poop!

Dad had already left for work by the time I came downstairs for breakfast. Mom, Nana, and Pop were sitting at the kitchen table drinking coffee.

Mom looked at her watch and sprang into motion. She hurried to the staircase, saying loudly as she looked up, "Emerson, come downstairs, please." Silence. "Now! Hurry up, or you'll be late for school and I'll be late for work."

Emmie came downstairs with the nail polish Nana and Pop had given her. "I'm going to show everyone what I got for graduation for show-and-tell."

"Great idea," said Mom, who was distracted, looking through her purse for the keys she was always looking for. "But don't open it," she added, making sure Emmie met her eyes and was paying attention. "If it makes a mess, Ms. Jerome will take it away and you won't have it for graduation. Go grab your backpack. Kiss Nana and Pop." Mom held up the keys she'd finally found as if they were a trophy. "Got 'em."

Then she turned to me. "Nana and Pop are hanging out with you today. Thank you for your help," she told them. "I'm going to try to get home early. Call me if you need anything."

Emmie raced out with her backpack. The door to the garage closed behind them, and I watched from the window as the car backed out of the driveway and drove away.

It was suddenly quiet in the kitchen. "Can I cook you some breakfast? Do you want eggs?" Nana asked me.

"No, thanks. I'll just have some Froot Loops." I got a bowl and a spoon, then pulled the cereal out of the pantry and the milk from the fridge. As I was eating, I stared at the back of the box as if I cared about the ingredients so that I didn't have to talk. If I had my phone, it would have been so much easier to look busy.

"Do you want to read any of the paper?" Pop asked. I saw the headline about the Phillies losing last night. "Looks like it's going to be a long season for the Phils." He pushed the sports section across the table, which wobbled a little as usual. He frowned.

I didn't want to read the paper. I wanted to see *Phillies Nation* or the *Bleacher Report* on my phone.

I could tell Nana was staring at me. Man, this was going to be a long day.

When I was finished, I put the bowl and spoon in the sink and headed to the basement.

"Where are you going?" she asked.

"Um, I was going to play Madden."

"Who's Madden?"

She'd obviously never heard of the best

Xbox game there was—unlike Pop, who said, "Well, he was an NFL coach and TV announcer. But I'm guessing Ezra is going to play the Madden video game. Right, Ez?" He winked at me.

Pop was cool. Still, I didn't really want to talk, so I just said, "Yeah."

I was afraid Nana would try to get me to do something educational, so I hurried toward the basement, but she didn't stop me.

Maybe this wouldn't be as bad as I thought. I mean, yesterday had been horrible, but at least today I wasn't sitting in school. And then I thought about the kids who were mean, and my face got hot, and I was *really* glad I wasn't there.

I played Madden for what must have been hours. I was about to check the time on my phone, but as soon as I reached into my pocket, I remembered again that I didn't have it.

The clock on the DVR said 9:48. Wow. It was earlier than I thought.

I was getting a little bored, but I still didn't want to talk to Nana and Pop, so I switched over to FIFA. I played that for a long time too. 10:11. I switched over to watching TV, but there was nothing good on. I had no phone to scroll through, and I was bored out of my mind.

Finally, I started feeling a little hungry, so I turned off the TV and went back upstairs. Nana was standing at the sink, wearing Mom's long yellow dish gloves and washing the dishes before loading them into the dishwasher. I didn't get the whole "wash before you dishwash" concept, which I argued about every time I had to do the dishes, but Mom and Dad seemed to think, like Nana did, that the dishwasher by itself wouldn't get them clean enough. Still, no way would I *ever* wear gloves. Especially not bright yellow ones.

I wondered where Pop was, and then I noticed his legs sticking out from under the kitchen table.

Nana turned around and saw me looking. "Oh, he's just fixing the table."

With that, Pop slid out from under the table. He stood up, held a screwdriver like a trophy, pushed down on the table, which didn't move, and said proudly, "Not wobbly anymore." Then he looked at me. "What's the story, Morning Glory?" I wondered how old you had to be to start saying stuff like that.

"I'm a little hungry," I said.

Those were magic words for Nana. Her face brightened. "Oh!" she said as she peeled off the rubber gloves. "There are peaches in the refrigerator. They look so good and juicy."

That made me think of the peach butt picture, and suddenly I wasn't hungry anymore. "No thanks, Nana." She looked sad, so I added, "I'll just take a banana."

"What are you up to?"

"Nothing." I sat down at the un-wobbly table.

"We could play a board game," she offered.

"No thanks."

"Well, I need to go to the drugstore," she said. "I forgot to pack my shower cap." I had no idea what she was talking about. Was it like a baseball cap? Why would you wear it in the shower? And why would they sell it at the drugstore? The only hats I'd ever seen them sell there were sets of winter beanies and mittens, but it was June.

Pop saw I was confused. "That's a cap Nana puts on her head in the shower. It keeps the water from messing up her hairdo." He rolled his eyes.

"Do you want to go with me?" she asked. I definitely didn't want to buy a shower cap, and they didn't sell sports equipment or any good toys there.

I shook my head. "No thanks, Nana."

"It's a beautiful day outside," said Pop. "How's about you and me take Lucy on a walk?" Lucy was lying on the floor, and she looked up when she heard her name.

I had nothing better to do. I shrugged my

shoulders and tried to push away the thoughts about why I was suspended. "OK."

Pop went to the mudroom for the leash. Lucy knew what that meant, and she got up and started wagging her tail.

We all left the house together. Nana had her keys in her hand. I saw that when she got into the car, she adjusted the mirror down so she could see herself. She fluffed up her hair, then adjusted the mirror back, fastened her seat belt, and drove away. I rolled my eyes at Pop, just like he had done. He smiled at me and messed my hair a little.

Pop held Lucy's leash, and we walked down the street together. He didn't talk for a while, and I didn't either. I could hear the birds and cars in the distance.

"Nice day," he finally said.

"Yeah," I said. I hoped we wouldn't have to "have a talk." I was worried he'd tell me I'd done something really stupid and he was dis-appointed in me, as if I didn't already know.

"As long as it doesn't get too humid, the heat isn't bad."

"Yeah."

We kept walking for a while without saying anything.

"Wanna talk about it?" Pop asked.

I shook my head. "No."

He nodded. "I get it. Your mom didn't want to talk about it when she got in trouble either. She was a little older than you, but not much. I think she was in seventh grade."

I looked at him. Mom in trouble? No way.

"In fact, what she did was kind of like what you did."

That didn't make any sense. "Mom told me she didn't have a phone until she was in high school. How'd she take pictures of—"

"Oh, no, this was middle school. She didn't have a phone yet. She passed a note in class. It said mean things about another girl and called her some very bad words. I didn't even know she knew those words. The teacher caught her.

Nana and I had to go in and pick her up from school."

"What were the words?" I wanted to hear.

"Oh, I don't remember," said Pop, but I knew he was lying.

"Did the other girl find out?"

"No, but because of what was in that note, the teacher sent your mom and her friend to the principal."

My mom, going to the principal's office! "Did she get suspended?"

"Not suspended, but she had to stay after school every day for two weeks. One of those days was the Friday that her Girl Scout troop was going on a weekend camp-out, so she had to miss it." Lucy was pulling on the leash. "Easy, girl! Anyway," he continued, "I think the worst part of it was that she'd passed the note to her best friend, who also got in trouble—and she hadn't done anything. They didn't talk for the rest of the year, and even after they made up, it was never the same."

It was hard to believe that Mom had ever done anything like that. She was the one always talking about being considerate. She was the one who always said, "There's no need for name-calling." One time when I called Emmie a "dum-dum" and made her cry, I got sent right to my room.

But still. Passing a note, even if it had bad words, wasn't as bad as what I had done, and no one else had known except her best friend and the teacher and the principal. And Nana and Pop.

The whole school knew about me. More than the whole school. The police. Anyone else who saw. And it had almost gone viral.

"So?" I said to Pop. "No one really knew. That's not so bad."

"You might not think so, but it really was. She had always been a good student, and now she had detention. Her troop had been preparing for the camping trip all year, and now she couldn't go. And the worst part was that she lost her best friend. It was terrible for your mother. She really hadn't thought about what would happen after that note left her hand."

Lucy stopped to smell something. Whenever she stopped on walks, there was no use pulling her because it was like trying to drag a boulder, so we just stood there waiting for her to move.

"She probably thought she was being funny, and that her friend would like her even more," I said.

Pop turned away from Lucy and looked right at me. "I think that's exactly what she thought. And it turned out that wanting to be liked so much that she did something she shouldn't have cost her the friendship she valued most."

I thought of Lilly, and Jasper, and Danny.

"I know it seems awful right now, Ez," he went on in a softer voice. "It's serious, for sure. But I wanted you to know about your mom because, just like you, she was humiliated, but she got over it. So will you. This, too, shall pass." I hoped he was right.

Just then the leash jerked in Pop's hands. Lucy was lying on her back, scooching around on a pile of another dog's poop as if it was the best thing ever. She wiggled around, and I caught a whiff of the stinky poop smell. It was so strong I could almost taste it.

"Lucy!" Pop yelled, pulling on the leash to get her off it. Too late.

"Ewwwwww," I said, holding my nose.

Pop made a face. "Holy cow, that's a lot of poop! How'd we not notice that? I'm not even sure that was made by a dog. Maybe a horse."

Lucy looked up at us and wagged her tail.

"Well, I guess we know what we'll be doing when we get home," he said. "Which we should do now."

I held my nose the whole way. We stood in the front yard, and Pop told me to go inside and get some dog shampoo and the gloves Nana had used to wash the dishes.

Since Lucy usually went to the groomer's, we didn't have dog shampoo, so I grabbed

Mom's Finesse, which had the strongest smell of all our shampoos. It smelled good—definitely better than dog poop. They should have put that in the ads.

When I got back outside, Pop was still holding Lucy's leash, but he had dragged over Emmie's wading pool and was filling it with water from the hose. When the pool was full, he went to turn off the spigot, and as soon as he did, Lucy jumped right in—she loves water. I handed Pop the shampoo and gloves, and he handed me the leash. He put on the gloves, then bent over Lucy and squeezed out some Finesse.

It took her a second to realize there was something on her back—other than the poop, I guess—and she began to pull away. I was holding the leash to keep her in the pool while Pop massaged the shampoo into her fur.

"Darn," he said. "I forgot to tell you to get something to rinse her off with." He cupped his gloved hands and dipped them into the pool.

Lucy was really pulling. "Hold on tight, Ez," Pop said.

I was trying. She was soaked, so now she was covered with super-wet, smelly poop. Suddenly, she stopped squirming and sat down, so I took that second to get a better grip on the leash, which was beginning to slip out of my hand.

And then Lucy stood up and shook her whole body. The dirty water, shampoo lather, and bits of poop showered me and Pop.

I didn't get too much of it because I was a few feet back, but Pop was standing right next to her. I think some water and maybe shampoo and poop got in his mouth. He made a noise that sounded like he was both coughing and yelling, and I dropped the leash.

Lucy took off and ran under the bush.

Just then, Nana came up the driveway. One look at us, and she was out of the car.

"What in blazes . . ." She started laughing so hard she had to bend down and put her hands on her knees. When she caught her breath, she said, "I'm thinking you boys should take a shower before lunch."

"Ya think?" asked Pop, the way I say, "duh," when someone says something really obvious.

Nana pressed her lips together so she wouldn't start laughing again.

Punishment

After we'd cleaned up the yard and showered—even Lucy—Nana made lunch. When she started to rinse the dishes, she realized why the gloves were gone and shot a look at Pop.

"Yeah," he said. "You might want to go to the supermarket to get another pair of those gloves." I tried not to laugh. "Also, I think they might be running low on Finesse, so you should probably pick up some of that too."

I sat at the kitchen table, not sure what to do next. I was bored playing video games by myself. I couldn't text my friends since they were in school, and I didn't have a phone anyway. Even if I could, I didn't know if they'd want to talk to me since they might be mad I got them in trouble.

It would have been OK if I could have played Roblox or Minecraft or Pokémon Go or even checkers on my phone . . . but, again, I didn't have my phone.

So, yeah, I was bored. And sad. And mad. I gave up and just sat there. Pop was doing the crossword puzzle in the newspaper and didn't notice.

When she was finished with the dishes, Nana turned around and said, "You know what, Ezra? Since I'm going to the store to get dishwashing gloves and shampoo, why don't you come with me? I could use your help picking out a special snack that you and Emmie might like."

That was all the encouragement I needed. There was nothing else happening, and I had never managed to get Mom to buy the

Entenmann's donuts with the crumble on top, but I was sure I could convince Nana. And once she'd bought them, no way Mom could refuse to let us have them.

Plus, everyone was at school, so no kids would see me.

Nana bought the donuts—two boxes, even—and I was pretty psyched until we got home and I saw both Mom's and Dad's cars in the driveway. Mom had said she'd be home early, but Dad's car too? That wasn't good.

Bags in hand, Nana had started up the driveway, but she turned around when she realized I wasn't following her. I did *not* want to go in there. But I had to, so I took a deep breath and walked as slowly as I could.

Mom and Dad were in the family room talking to Pop when we came in.

Pop stood up. "Here, Gail, let me help you get that bag into the kitchen." He took it from her hands. "I told them"—he gestured toward Mom and Dad—"that I'd barbecue tonight, but they don't have any propane, so I'm going to get some. Why don't you come along?"

"I'll go with you," I offered, even though I knew it wouldn't work.

"No, let Nana and Pop go by themselves, Ezra," Dad said. "We need to talk to you."

Now my heart was really pounding, and my hands started shaking a little. I sat down on the comfy chair next to the couch. Nana kissed the top of my head but didn't say anything

After the door closed, I hugged my knees to my chest and put my head inside my arms like I was an armadillo making myself into a ball. My eyes were covered, but I heard Dad say, "We heard from Detective Kelly, Ez."

I looked up.

"They completed the investigation, and she told us that there was only the one picture that we knew would be there." I knew that was all they'd find, but I still sighed with relief.

Dad nodded and kept talking. "So that's good. Detective Kelly said we'd get login information soon for the internet safety class you'll have to take online this summer."

Wait, what? "I have to go to school in the summer?"

"It's not school—it's just one class," he reassured me. "It's one night a week for eight weeks, so you can still go to the sports camps you're signed up for during the day." Phew.

Whatever. It was fine, I guess. But he wasn't done. "Once you've finished the class, they'll need to send a letter to Detective Kelly, and then she said they could close the investigation and put the matter behind us. So it'll be over before you get to middle school."

That could've been much worse, I thought.

Then it got much worse.

Dad stopped talking, and Mom took over. "That's what Detective Kelly had to say, but we also heard from Mr. Brubaker. You remember he said that there would be a separate school consequence?" She looked at me, and I braced myself. "Since school is so close to being over, you'll be suspended for the rest of the year. You'll get your assignments from the homework portal and send them in by email. He said that if you finish all the work you're supposed to do, you'll get to march in graduation."

I let out a deep breath. My parents were upset I had gotten suspended, but it was only for a few days, and it meant I didn't have to deal with anyone from school.

"Get" to march in graduation though? As if that was somehow a privilege? They would all be there. Alex elbowing me, and Carter laughing—and that stupid Molly Murtaugh making fun of me—still made me hot with anger and embarrassment. I prayed that if I did see them, I wouldn't want to cry every time I thought about what happened.

At least my friends would be there. When I thought about that, though, I wasn't so sure I wanted to see some of *them* either—especially not Matthew. The whole thing was his fault. I mean, yeah, I took the photo, and I was going to post it, but I didn't. *Matthew* was the one who sent it. And he'd called me a beaver butt, so what could I do?

"Ezra, did you hear me?" Mom's voice was sharp. I hadn't, actually. "I said that Mr. Brubaker said you won't be allowed to go on the trip to Dorney Park."

"*What?* But that's so unfair! I've been waiting to go to Dorney Park since *first grade*." I was even angrier now—and there was nothing I could do about it. "Everyone else gets to go except me? I'm the only kid getting punished?"

Mom shook her head. "Mr. Brubaker said a total of fifteen kids had the photo. They've collected the phones, and now it's been deleted from all of them. One of those kids showed it to a trusted adult, so that kid wasn't punished. The rest will all take the class you're taking.

"Luckily, after the photo was sent from your phone, only three of the kids who got it forwarded it. One of them doesn't go to Hughes anymore, so Mr. Brubaker isn't in charge of what happens to them." I knew that was Peyton. It didn't matter if he was mad at me because I probably wouldn't see him anyway.

That left Matthew and Lilly. Mom continued, "One of them lost the Dorney Park trip too. But the third kid was Lilly—who only sent it back to you and then deleted it—so even though she'll have to take the class too, she'll be able to go to Dorney Park."

I wondered what Matthew and Lilly were feeling. I was glad Matthew had lost the Dorney Park trip—he deserved it!—but he was probably mad at me, which was stupid because I had more of a right to be mad at *him*. Either way, I didn't want to be on Matthew's bad side.

I was glad Lilly could go on the trip, but was she mad at me too because she'd gotten mixed up in the whole thing? I wanted to ask more, but I didn't. Mom must have known I was worried because she said, "I talked to Mrs. Mensh after we got off the phone with the principal."

"You called her, or she called you?" I was

really hoping Mom hadn't made it worse by calling Lilly's mom to talk about me.

"She called me. She felt bad about the whole situation, and she was worried about you. She said Lilly was too."

"Is Lilly mad she has to take the class over the summer?"

"She didn't say. She just said Lilly hoped you were OK." That was good. And at least I knew that if I had to see people at graduation, I'd be standing next to her.

"And one more thing," said Dad. One more thing and one more thing. This would never end.

"We know this could have been much worse. Mom and I realize we messed up because we never told you about how to use your phone safely, and we're sorry." He and Mom shared a look. "So we've made a decision. Once Detective Kelly returns it, we're going to keep it and only give it back to you *after* you finish the class. This summer, you'll have to use the landline like you used to—and like we did in prehistoric days when we were your age."

They were keeping my phone? For *eight weeks?* It had only been gone a day, and I missed it more than anything. I couldn't imagine what summer would be like. All these years of waiting, and when I finally got a phone, I only had it for two weeks before they took it away.

But it was worse than just not having games. Since I was the last in my group to get a phone, I knew how left out you felt when everyone else was talking about a new app or texting each other. And how, when you were just standing around with nothing to do, you could play on your phone or pretend to be busy with something else so you didn't look dumb.

And who cared that I could talk on a landline? My friends didn't call each other. We texted. They'd forget I even existed if I wasn't part of a group text when they all decided to hang out together. If I even still had friends.

Mom and Dad looked at me. "Anything you want to say?" asked Dad.

I took a deep breath. "Please, can I get my phone back? I swear I will *never* post pictures of myself again."

"I believe you, Ezra," he said, "but there are consequences for what you did. And one of them is that you need to finish the entire class before you can have your phone."

It wasn't fair! I thought about arguing. I knew I shouldn't have taken the picture or shown it to anyone, but—and I hated to admit it—I knew deep down that telling my parents it was Matthew's fault wouldn't convince them.

Anyway, I didn't want to see anything people were saying about me. I was honestly kind of relieved that I couldn't. I could pretend I was invisible to anyone who wasn't my actual friend.

We all just sat quietly, and then Emmie's car pool pulled up, and she came bursting through the door.

"Can I get more nail polish?" she asked breathlessly. "I don't have any left."

"What? Why?" Mom sounded like she was getting mad.

"It's not my fault that it spilled on Analyn."

"Before you left for school this morning, what did I tell you about not opening the bottle?" They went into the kitchen, Mom still scolding and Emmie saying it wasn't her fault that Analyn wanted to try it on, as if Analyn was the one who made her do something she knew she shouldn't.

It sounded so much like what I had been thinking that I realized Analyn was like Matthew, and I was kind of like Emmie, too easily convinced to do something I knew I shouldn't.

Getting Butterflies

Only a few days of school were left, and they seemed to last forever—and not in the good way vacation does when there's enough time to do everything, but in the bad, boring way when you can't wait for something to be over.

It was so bad I almost looked forward to doing my homework off the web portal. After I finished, Pop and I would take Lucy for a walk, and then I'd watch TV or play games.

When Emmie came home from school, I would help her collect caterpillars in the backyard. One of the chrysalises had turned clear, and you could see from its orange and black wings that it was going to be a monarch butterfly.

That's how bored I was. I was spending time with my sister on purpose and had started caring about butterflies.

One thing I *didn't* do was call my friends. No one called me either. And every day brought me closer to graduation when I would have to see everyone for the first time since I'd been suspended. Worried and bored: not a great combination.

On Monday, when Emmie went outside to check on her caterpillars, she started yelling. "Ezra! Come here! Look!" I ran outside, and she was holding up the bug container. "Look in the corner. The butterfly is out of the chrysalis!"

It was pretty cool, I had to say. You could see that the butterfly was outside the chrysalis, but its wings were still kind of folded up as if it were still inside.

Emmie rushed into the house even though she knew she wasn't supposed to bring the bug collector inside.

"Mom! Look," she cried. I followed her to see if Mom would think it was cool or if she would yell at her for bringing the caterpillars in the house—or maybe both.

But then I stopped short.

Since I was in the backyard, I hadn't heard any cars pull up, and I hadn't heard the doorbell ring. But now I saw Mom in the entry hall opening the front door for Lilly and her mom.

The three of them turned when Emmie came in yelling, so they saw me too. I was trapped.

"Look! The caterpillar emerged from the chrysalis and is now a butterfly!" she announced happily.

I couldn't move. Lilly and our moms looked inside the bug collector, and they did seem impressed. But then my mom said, "Emmie, that's great, but you know the rule: no bugs in the house."

"But it's not a bug—it's a butterfly." She had a point.

"Yes, and it—and I—will be much happier

if it is outside where it can fly free once its wings dry."

Emmie stopped talking and just blinked a couple of times. It was clear she hadn't thought this through. Once caterpillars became full-fledged butterflies, they flew away, and she wouldn't have them anymore. She looked into the bug collector a little sadly.

"Emmie, go outside, please."

"Fine," she said, and shuffled out. I didn't know if I should follow her or not.

"Hey, Ezra," Mom said, "why don't you and Lilly go with her to make sure she's not too sad about setting the butterflies free."

I looked at Lilly. She nodded, and we went outside.

"Hey," I said.

"Hey. You're lucky you didn't have to sit through boring school all day." She didn't sound mad.

"Well, it's been pretty boring around here too."

Before she could answer, the back door opened again—and this time Jasper came outside.

"Yo!" Jasper called. Then he saw Lilly and stopped dead. "Whoa," he blurted out.

Lilly looked at him, her head tilted. "Whoa?"

"I mean, oh," he managed. "I—I mean, yo. I mean, hi."

"Oh," said Lilly, turning red. "Hi."

"Hi," said Jasper, also turning red.

"Wow," I said. And I thought *I* was the awkward one. I was so happy to see Jasper and Lilly even though it was clear they were mostly happy to see each other.

"I didn't know you guys were coming over." My voice snapped them out of their trance.

Jasper spoke first. "My mom said it was OK for me to come over since she said my moping around was getting on her nerves."

Then Lilly said, "My mom said that your mom invited me to come over. She said you'd been spending a lot of time alone."

Now it was my turn to turn red. "Yeah, well, I'm not getting my phone back for eight weeks, so I couldn't really text anyone. And I wasn't sure if anyone would still want to text me anyway."

"I do," said Jasper.

"Me too," Lilly said.

I felt like I could breathe for the first time in days.

"Hey," Jasper said to Lilly, "Maybe we could text each other when we want to talk to Ezra."

"Oh, yeah, that's a great idea," she said.

It didn't sound like a great idea. What it sounded like was a great excuse for Jasper to text Lilly and then for neither of them to talk to me. But I was so happy to hear they were still my friends and would text me when I finally got my phone back that I didn't call him out about it.

Then what I'd said finally registered. "Wait," Jasper said, "why aren't you getting your phone back for eight weeks? We all got ours back now that they've finished investigating."

"Because that's how long the class is—that online class about internet security that we have to take—and my parents aren't letting me have my phone back until it's over. And I don't even know when that will be because I don't know when the class is supposed to start. Do you?"

"I don't know," said Jasper.

"Next Thursday night," said Lilly at the same time. "I guess we'll all be in the same class together, even if it's just online."

"Uh, no, I'm not in the class," Jasper muttered.

"Why not?" I asked. "I thought we all had to take it."

Now he looked away. "Well, um, I got a text from Matthew with no message, just the photo—I didn't know what it was, or that you guys were looking at it during lunch. It seemed weird to me, so I showed it to Josephine, and she showed it to my mom. I didn't find out until later that it was one that you took, or that you'd get in trouble. I'm so sorry, Ezra," he said, finally meeting my eyes. "I didn't know what to do or whether to tell you when I heard you got suspended, and I wasn't sure if you'd ever talk to me again," he finished in a rush.

It took a second to sink in. *Jasper was the reason I got in trouble.*

"Are you mad at me?" he asked. "I didn't believe Matthew when he said it was you. I knew that all the other pictures you'd taken were fake. But it looked so real that I thought maybe it was someone's actual butt, so I asked Josephine what she thought. And then I couldn't stop what happened next."

"I couldn't either," I said.

I believed him. I knew Jasper would never want to get me in trouble. He was my best friend, the only one I always knew I could count on to stand up for me—unlike all those other people I thought wanted to be my friends but were just waiting until I messed up. I didn't want to lose my best friend the way Mom had lost hers.

We were all quiet.

Finally, I said, "Maybe it's better it got stopped when it did and got deleted from everyone's phones. The worst part—I mean, aside from getting suspended—was all the popular kids making fun of me." It felt hard but good to tell them. "And they weren't doing it because I got in trouble, but because so many people had already heard about my picture, which wasn't your fault," I told Jasper. "It was mine. I took the picture, and I showed it."

Lilly broke in. "Those kids are so mean! The boys *and* the girls. They only think about themselves, and not how they make other people feel. But at least you know the good part about how self-centered they are—by the time we start middle school, they'll be talking about how cute they all look and who's partying with who, and they won't even pay any attention to you anyway."

Another weight lifted off me. Lilly was right. The popular kids would go back to ignoring me—and although I wouldn't have believed it a month ago, that thought had me super psyched.

I smiled, and then because I smiled, Jasper smiled. And then so did Lilly. And then Jasper and Lilly started smiling at each other. I rolled my eyes a little.

"Look!" yelled Emmie. "Come quick!"

The three of us ran over. The butterfly's wings looked much bigger than when it had first come out of the chrysalis. It had even begun to flap a little. I wished I had my phone.

We watched for a few minutes, and then Emmie looked at me. I nodded.

She slowly opened the container so the butterfly could get out, but it didn't move right away. It stayed inside, slowly moving its wings. We waited, and then it finally came up out of the top and began to flutter away.

"Be safe," Emmie whispered. We all watched

it as it flew upward then disappeared into a group of trees where we couldn't see it anymore.

"I hope it remembers me and comes back to visit," she said.

"Real friends do," said Lilly.

It Ends

OK. This was it. Graduation. As I pulled open the school door, I took a deep breath and prayed that Jasper or Lilly would be standing there.

Of course, the first person I saw was Carter Williams.

A million people were crowded inside, but just my luck—right in front of me was Carter. He was like the last person I ever wanted to face again. Except for Alex. And Molly. And anyone who was whispering about me. And anyone who got in trouble because of the picture and might still be mad at me.

More than anything I wanted to be invisible, like I used to be, and never have to deal with any of them. But Carter was right up there at the top of the long list.

My heart started pounding a mile a minute. I tried to hang back behind Nana, but she wasn't really tall enough, so I inched over toward Dad.

Huge mistake. While I was checking to make sure I was hidden, Dad spotted Carter's dad, who he hadn't seen in years.

"Jeff!" my dad practically yelled, and there was nothing I could do to stop him.

Both Carter and his dad looked over at us. I wanted to run, but it was too late. Mr. Williams gave my dad a huge smile and a hearty hand-shake. He was with a girl who had long hair and a piercing in the side of her nose. She was wearing a short dress and high boots that came all the way over her knees.

"Paul!" Carter's dad said to my dad. "How's it hanging? You look great!" He must have noticed Dad looking at the girl with him. "I don't think you've met my girlfriend, Brittany. Brit, this is Paul Miller. He and I used to play golf together. Paul, Brit worked in our marketing department before she went back to grad school."

I didn't know where to look. I tried to stick my hands in the pockets of my new khakis, but they were sewn shut. I looked down and pretended Carter wasn't standing right there.

But then a miracle happened. Because I was looking down, I had a view mostly of his shoes and legs—but I also saw that his fly was unzipped. And even better—I could actually see that he was wearing robot underpants. Like a little kid.

He was supposed to be the coolest kid in school, and he wore robot underpants. He was laughing at me, and *he* wore robot underpants! If I could find Matthew and tell him, for sure he'd forget about Beaver Butt and maybe not be mad at me, and instead move on to making fun of Carter, the way the girls got tired of making fun of Sophie Bodinny.

Today wasn't so awful after all.

Right then, the crowd kind of parted because a woman was making a beeline right toward us. It was Carter's mom. She stood next to Carter and gave his dad a really mad look.

"Nice of you to show up for your kid for once—not that you could be bothered the last three times you said you'd visit," she said. Her voice was like a mean knife. She looked at Brittany and then back at Carter's dad. "Guess you managed to find yourself a babysitter." She rolled her eyes. "Good. You need one."

Brittany was turning bright red. She bent down to pull her boots, which were kind of saggy, back up over her knees.

That's when I saw the look on Carter's face.

I knew that look, when you were trying

hard not to cry. Yes, I really wanted people to make fun of someone other than me, but that look made me so sad for him. I suddenly remembered when we used to play superheroes together. Right now he looked like he did then when he was a little kid, and I guess he sometimes thought he still was one, with the robot underpants and all.

And then I felt like *I* wanted to cry. For him, for me, for all the stuff that had happened.

So I moved out from behind Dad. The adults didn't notice because they were still staring at each other. Carter saw, but I could tell he wasn't thinking about me because his eyes were blank.

I leaned in and cupped my hand over his ear so no one could hear me. He stepped back a little because he was surprised, and I knew it seemed weird, but this was private.

"Fix your zipper," I whispered.

He didn't say anything. He didn't even look at me. He just turned around, and I could see from how his head dropped and his shoulders moved that he was zipping up. When he turned back around, he nodded just a tiny bit.

At that exact second, Mr. Brubaker's voice came over the loudspeaker.

"All fifth-graders, please go to the cafeteria to line up. Guests, please take your seats in the auditorium."

It was chaos. Kids ran toward the cafeteria. All the fifth-grade teachers were already in there, trying to shush people who were showing each other their souvenir Dorney Park bracelets and keychains. Without drawing any attention to myself, I found my place in line.

Whew! Lilly was already there. "Hey," she said.

"Hey," I said.

"You OK?" she asked.

"Yeah, I guess."

Out of the corner of my eye, I saw Molly Murtaugh staring. Jasper wasn't there yet, so she was standing by herself, and I could tell she wanted to say something.

"Hey, butthead." I didn't turn around. "Hey, butthead," she said louder, like it was so hilarious the first time.

Lilly glared at her. "Shut up, Molly. You're not as funny as you think you are."

Molly must have been surprised because she was quiet for a second, but then she said, "You're not as funny as you think *you* are!"

"Good comeback," Lilly said sarcastically, turned back around, and rolled her eyes. She was awesome.

When Jasper finally appeared, I wasn't sure what he was going to say.

"Hey," he said, nodding at me. "Sup?"

"Hey," I said. He smiled at me, just normal. I smiled back.

We could hear "Pomp and Circumstance" starting. The line began to move, and we left the cafeteria two by two, marched down the hallway, and entered the back of the auditorium.

I kept my eyes forward as Lilly and I walked down the aisle.

I took my seat as the kids continued to file in. I was really praying no one would hit the back of my head as they walked by or say anything mean. All I wanted was for nobody to notice I was there.

Kid after kid went by, keeping their eyes forward. Then Carter walked past. He turned for a second and looked at me, gave a quick nod, and kept on walking.

I breathed out hard because I was so relieved.

●●●

When the ceremony was over, all the fifth-graders went back to the cafeteria, where cookies and juice were set out for us and our guests. Everyone was taking pictures in front of the sign that said, "Congratulations, Graduates!"

Jasper's mom came over and said, "I'd love

to get a picture of the boys together." Jasper put his arm over my shoulder.

As his mom was focusing, he said, "I guess this is the end. Get it? The *end?*" and he pointed to his butt. I didn't say anything. "What? Too soon?" he asked, laughing.

Much too soon, as far as I was concerned. No buts about it.

Afterword

Like Ezra's mom, I sent a mean note about a girl in my class to my best friend in elementary school, and my teacher saw the note being passed and confiscated it. She called us up to the front of the class and yelled at us. It's an incident that still fills me with shame both because I'd written such mean and thoughtless things and also because when the teacher confronted us, I didn't own up to the fact that I had written it at the time, which is why the teacher punished my best friend too, even though she hadn't done anything wrong. It was also mortifying because everyone in the class witnessed the fact that I got in trouble although

I can almost guarantee no one else who was in the class at the time has any recollection of it today.

The lucky thing for me was the teacher didn't read the note out loud, and it was written on a piece of notebook paper, not in an email, so it wasn't something that got out on social media. Not everyone is so lucky when they send messages. I think that even smart, thoughtful people—adults *and* kids—don't know or don't think about the ways that something they send electronically, even something really small, can come back to haunt them. That's why I wanted to tell the story of a really great kid who makes a really big mistake.

When something like what happened to Ezra happens to a kid in real life, there are legal consequences and school consequences—and social consequences that can greatly affect self-esteem. Basically, it seems like the end of the world.

What adults have—what kids have as they

get older—is the life experience to understand that even a situation that seems terrible at the moment will seem less bad when you look back. Every adult I know can think of something incredibly embarrassing they did when they were a kid or a teenager. And maybe the consequences *were* awful. But I can't think of a single one who can honestly say, "And because of it, my life changed forever." In the words of Ezra's grandfather, "This, too, shall pass."

If there's one thing I want readers to take from this book, it's this: Avoid sending out pictures or texts or emails that could hurt you or others. But if you do make a mistake and send something you regret, it won't always feel as horrible as it does when it first happens.

Things do get better. Please remember that.

Acknowledgments

This book would not have been possible without the guidance, support, and creativity of my sister, Robin Epstein, to whom I am truly grateful. I'm also incredibly indebted to Dan Ehrenhaft, an extremely talented writer in his own right, who acted as a reader, editor, advocate, and publisher to bring this story to life. I was fortunate to have the opportunity to work with the supremely talented Sharyn November, who managed to sharpen Ezra's character without ever losing his voice.

I would not have had the courage or the space to write this book were it not for Marty Judge Jr., Marty Judge III, Brian Anderson, Katy

Wiercinski, and all of my friends at The Judge Group Inc., who have encouraged me personally and professionally.

My friend and fellow author Lynn Rosen suggested I join the Society of Children's Book Writers and Illustrators (SCBWI), which proved to be a crucial piece of advice. My esteemed local SCBWI cohort, including Steve Silbiger, Tina Holt, Marilyn (Molly) Lorenz, Connie Gallagher, Sara Bates, Theresa Cocci, Matthew Bloome, and Kathy Spall, is an incredibly helpful, perceptive, and talented group of authors and illustrators, whose observations changed the book for the much, much better.

To ensure that the legal and judicial aspects were accurate, I consulted Judge Risa Furman, Judge Wendy Demchick-Alloy, and Judge Bill Maruszczak, who work every day to make the world a safer place for children. I also relied on, and am thankful for, the insight of law enforcement agents Detective Connie Marinello, Upper Moreland Police Chief Andy

Block, Detective Sergeant Jim Kelly, and Detective Frank Gallagher.

I am incredibly indebted to the teachers, administrators, and staff at Lower Merion School District for their help with this project, and for all they do every day to educate not only the students but also the parents on how to be kind and successful human beings. Principals Scott Weinstein and Sean Hughes are shining examples of how to foster a nurturing school environment, and they have left their mark on all those who have passed through the halls of their schools.

The opportunity to observe kids in their natural habitat—on the playground—at Arrowhead Day Camp was also hugely helpful, and for that I thank Aunt Ellen, Uncle Howie, and the entire Arrowhead family. In addition, Alexa and Josh Bloom and Tim and Jack Reymann helped remind me how a real kid looks, acts, and, most importantly, texts. Their contributions were invaluable.

Without a doubt, my husband and soul mate, Len Feldman, gave me the greatest gifts of all: the gift of his constant love and support and the gift of our amazing children. To Len, Maddie, Benjy, Eli, Jared, and also Callie: nothing I've done would have been either imaginable or meaningful without the joy you have brought me.

Q&A with Author
Amy E. Feldman

What inspired you to write *Ezra Exposed*?

A few years ago, a friend reached out because he'd gotten a call he never would have imagined in his worst nightmare: the police wanted to ask questions about his eighth-grade son. It turned out that his son had been involved with a group of boys exchanging nude photos of themselves with a group of girls. My friend didn't realize that disseminating lewd photos of a minor is a crime, period. In certain states, a thirteen-year-old can be held liable for trafficking in child pornography.

While I am a lawyer with specific expertise in the intersection of law, technology, and education, I know that my friend also reached out for a deeper reason. He wanted help with how to open up a conversation about sexting, about issues of shame and responsibility—and the legal ramifications—without terrifying his son. What I know: books always help as introductions to delicate but absolutely crucial conversations. And that was the spark that compelled me to write Ezra's story.

I hope that, above all, *Ezra Exposed* is entertaining. I also hope that it can provide real legal education in an age-appropriate way. My dream is that it will make kids (and their parents, as well as their teachers) laugh, open discussions, and allow tweens of all backgrounds to see themselves in a boy who loves to draw mustaches on his face and make his friends laugh—and to know that no matter how exposed a kid may feel, everyone has rights and responsibilities, helping them understand that things can get better.

What inspired you to be a writer in the first place?

I have always loved reading. I was the type of kid who used to spend lunch in the library in elementary school because it was my favorite place in the school. As I started my career in the law, I felt that communication and storytelling were really underappreciated parts of the craft of getting people to understand your side of the matter and winning the other side over. So when I started to do segments on the radio and on TV, I felt it was very important to humanize legal concepts with real-world examples of how the laws affect people as a means to get the audience to listen.

When it comes to why I wrote Ezra's story in particular, I felt like I had to because he was calling to me. I can't really explain how the concept of teaching kids about technology became this book, except that I heard Ezra's voice in my head and felt compelled to write down what it was saying to me.

Do you know any kids like Ezra?

I know an actual kid to whom almost the exact same thing happened. When I started telling people about the book, they started telling me that they also know other kids to whom the same thing happened. But beyond the facts of what happened in the story, Ezra is a boy I know very well. He has a spark that I see in my own kids and in other children I've been lucky enough to know.

Who are the authors who've inspired you?

Karina Yan Glaser, who wrote the series The Vanderbeekers, has the amazing ability to show all the different kinds of personalities that can coexist in the same family—and to show that members of a family still love each other even when they don't always get along. It's something that I kept in mind when creating Ezra's relationship with his sister.

Barbara Park is a writing hero of mine. While the Junie B. Jones books are for a slightly younger reader, Junie's voice is so strong and personable that I tried to emulate it in Ezra's internal monologue.

Gordon Korman is probably the author who inspired me the most for this novel. I love his writing style because his characters are so brave and funny, and I love that he lets readers into the heads of all of them.

How would you describe *Ezra Exposed*?

Hmm. In a sentence?

A ten-year-old, who longs to be popular, posts pictures of things that look like butts online, until one post that goes viral comes back to bite him in his own.

Obviously, there's more to it. Ezra is a jokester. He draws mustaches on his face with a Sharpie. He has been known to shove french fries up his nose. When he gets a cell phone as a combination tenth-birthday/fifth-grade graduation present, his creativity goes into overdrive. He takes pictures of things that make him laugh, which are photos of things that look like butts. From chicken nuggets stuck together, to a peach he sees in his friend's lunch, Ezra discovers that he can see butts everywhere. Soon he starts posting the photos on social media for his friends to see, and that's when the trouble starts. The kids at school love them. Ezra has always felt upstaged—by his little sister at home, and by the popular kids at school. But as he gains followers, he suddenly sees what it feels like to be a popular kid.

Of course, fifth-graders don't have all the time in the world to look at funny pictures and follow those who post them. There's the little matter of having to go to school and do homework, which Ezra does reluctantly, including his not-so-great science fair project. When his geekiest friend, Zack, gets a much better grade on the project than he does—and seems to be on the path to becoming more popular than he is—Ezra gets worried that his popularity is waning. Goaded into showing his friends a photo that he isn't sure he should send, he soon learns the truth about his sudden surge in popularity and the consequences of not thinking before taking a picture and hitting send.

Any final thoughts?

Above all, I hope Ezra's story raises the thorny legal issues around texting without frightening kids his age. News stories abound on the arrests and suspensions of children as young as middle-school age who have violated the law or school policy through their use of technology to transmit messages or pictures. Never has the First Amendment been so fraught for students who know so much about how to use technology to send their messages, yet so little about the consequences once the messages have been sent.

Discussion Questions

1. Why do you think Ezra started making funny posts?

2. What does it mean to be popular? How do you know if you are popular?

3. Who are Ezra's friends? Who isn't Ezra's friend? How did Ezra's definition of "friend" change over the course of the book?

4. What do you consider the qualities that make someone a friend? Is there a difference between being a friend in person versus a friend online? Can they be the same?

5. Could Ezra have gotten into trouble for the posts that came before his actual butt photo? Should he have?

6. Which character or characters do you consider a hero in this story? Why?

7. Was Jasper right to show the photo to his babysitter, Josephine? Why or why not?

8. What would you say is the definition of a "trusted adult"? Do you have a trusted adult? If so, who?

9. What do you think will happen after the summer when Ezra starts middle school? Will kids still tease him about the photo? Why or why not? If someone teases him, what should he say?